Hello, Gorgeous!

Swept Up

GROSSET & DUNLAP
Published by the Penguin Group
Penguin Group (USA) Inc., 375 Hudson Street,
New York, New York 10014, USA
Penguin Group (Canada), 90 Eglinton Avenue East, Suite 700,
Toronto, Ontario M4P 2Y3, Canada
(a division of Pearson Penguin Canada Inc.)
Penguin Books Ltd., 80 Strand, London WC2R 0RL, England
Penguin Group Ireland, 25 St. Stephen's Green, Dublin 2, Ireland
(a division of Penguin Books Ltd.)
Penguin Group (Australia), 250 Camberwell Road, Camberwell, Victoria
3124, Australia (a division of Pearson Australia Group Pty. Ltd.)
Penguin Books India Pvt. Ltd., 11 Community Centre,
Panchsheel Park, New Delhi—110 017, India
Penguin Group (NZ), 67 Apollo Drive, Rosedale, Auckland 0632,
New Zealand (a division of Pearson New Zealand Ltd.)
Penguin Books (South Africa) (Pty.) Ltd., 24 Sturdee Avenue,
Rosebank, Johannesburg 2196, South Africa

Penguin Books Ltd., Registered Offices:
80 Strand, London WC2R 0RL, England

Text copyright © 2012 by Taylor Morris. Cover illustration copyright © 2012
by Anne Keenan Higgins. All rights reserved. Published by Grosset & Dunlap,
a division of Penguin Young Readers Group, 345 Hudson Street,
New York, New York 10014. GROSSET & DUNLAP is a trademark of
Penguin Group (USA) Inc. Printed in the U.S.A.

Library of Congress Cataloging-in-Publication Data is available.

ISBN 978-0-448-45529-7   10 9 8 7 6 5 4 3 2 1

Hello, Gorgeous!

Swept Up

BY TAYLOR MORRIS

GROSSET & DUNLAP
An Imprint of Penguin Group (USA) Inc.

CHAPTER 1

"Mickey, hello? Are you listening?"

At the sound of Kristen's voice, I looked up from staring at the nothingness of the cream carpet in Lizbeth's bedroom. It was Saturday night, and Kristen sat in front of the full-length mirror, waiting for me to work my magic.

"Sorry," I said. I began brushing her hair again. "Must have spaced out."

"You okay?" Lizbeth asked. She sat at her desk, a stack of magazines in front of her.

"Yeah," I said. "I'm fine."

I wasn't really. If you've ever had a fight with a friend then I bet you can understand. And I had no one to blame but myself. Eve was determined to never talk to me again, all because of my big mouth.

"You sure?" Kristen asked, looking at my reflection in the mirror.

"Yeah," I said, pulling the brush through her long, shiny hair. "Positive. Just thinking about how to do this look." I nodded toward the magazine beside us, opened to a style she wanted me to try for the dance on Friday. I made a deep part on the side of Kristen's head and brushed her hair over. Lizbeth kept her eyes on me for a moment longer before turning back to her magazine.

I didn't want to ruin our sleepover, our first without our friend—*my* friend—so I didn't say what had me spaced out. The truth was, the night felt empty without Eve. And if I couldn't fix things, this was the way they were going to be for the rest of seventh grade. And maybe our whole lives. The thought almost wrecked me.

"So, Mickey," Kristen said. "It's been a week and we still haven't heard the details about you and Kyle." Her smile stretched wall-to-wall as she asked, "Has he kissed you yet?"

"No!" I blurted out, ignoring the flash of heat on my cheeks and pulling a little too hard on Kristen's hair, making her cringe. Kissing already? We'd only just started hanging out.

"Have you *tried* to kiss him?" Kristen teased.

"No," I said firmly.

"Don't you *want* him to kiss you?" Kristen asked.

"Kristen," I huffed. "We're just hanging out. It's not that big of a deal."

"Sure," she said, a greedy grin on her face. "We believe you. Uh-huh."

"Hey," I said, pointing the brush to her face in the mirror. "Never egg on a girl who holds your hair in her hands."

She laughed. "Then I surrender."

I tried to laugh, too, but being at Lizbeth's without Eve was hard. Talking about Kyle was exciting, but I felt like a Ping-Pong ball bouncing between happiness over Kyle and sadness over Eve.

Here's the deal: Eve and Jonah were my two best friends who happened to like each other, and they started spending a lot of time together. Like, so much time together that they totally ignored everything and everyone else. I was pretty frustrated about it, so I came up with a plan to detach them from the hip. My goal was to remind them that hanging out with their own friends—like me and the girls—was actually a nice way to spend an evening. Except the plan blew up in my face when I altered the truth slightly, telling Jonah that Eve was upset and then telling Eve that Jonah didn't want to hang out with her.

Yeah, I know. It was a major bad-friend move.

It almost broke them up. It definitely caused them both a lot of heartache with each other and with me. And for sure none of it was necessary. I'd butted in where I never should have. Jonah has forgiven me, but that's Jonah—we've had plenty of ups and downs and stuff just rolls off him. But Eve felt hugely burned and said we needed to back off our friendship for a bit. Not exactly like a breakup, but a break nonetheless.

I was embarrassed by what I'd done, but I also desperately wanted to make it up to her. Eve was my friend—I hated having her mad at me. I hated that I'd done something to make her mad at me. I knew I could be a good friend—a better friend—if she'd just give me the chance to prove it. So even though it was scary, I tried talking to her last week. Just casual stuff, no deep conversations. Baby steps.

On Tuesday in English class, just before we took a quiz, Eve was digging frantically in her bag.

"Eve, hey," I whispered across the aisle. "Need a pen?"

She shook her head no and kept digging. I grabbed my bag and quickly got an extra pen.

"Here," I said, leaning across to her. She was one seat up so her back was to me. She didn't turn to look. "Eve."

Just as I was about to toss it onto her desk, Rebecca, a girl on the other side of Eve, offered her a pen, saving the day.

I put the pen back in my bag, trying not to feel stupid. Trying not to wonder if she had ignored me on purpose.

Each day at lunch Eve still sat with us, but she mostly talked to Jonah. She said hi to me; she even answered when I asked if she liked the lasagna special on Thursday ("I guess"), but it all felt flat and meaningless.

On the other hand, things with Kyle were going great. We just got along so well, and he was so cute and sweet. And while I loved hanging out with Kristen and Lizbeth, talking about boys and doing hair, I had to admit—at least to myself—that I really missed Eve. It was like I missed her as much as I liked Kyle, if that makes any sense.

"You don't have to give us the details about Kyle if you don't want to," Lizbeth said as I thought about how to execute the style on Kristen's hair. "But we are curious."

"*Extremely* curious," Kristen added.

Before Lizbeth could ask another question, her phone buzzed with a new text. I was relieved. With everything that was going on in my head, I wasn't sure I was ready to spill it all only to have the girls pick it apart.

"It's from Matthew," Lizbeth said, reading her phone.

"What does it say?" Kristen asked.

"Okay," Lizbeth said, reading. "He just says that *Tombstone* is the best Western of all time."

Both girls looked disappointed. "What does that have to do with anything?" Kristen asked.

"They must be watching movies at Tobias's house," Lizbeth said, dropping the phone on her desk and going back to her magazine.

Kristen shook her head. "Back to Mickey, please. Come on, tell us everything!"

"You don't have to tell us everything," Lizbeth said, eyeing Kristen. "We just want to know how it's going. Like, is it good? Are you happy?"

I looked at their expectant faces, Kristen's a bit more eager (ravenous?) than Lizbeth's friendly, concerned smile.

"Yeah," I said, unable to suppress the grin creeping across my face as I thought about Kyle. "Things are going well. He's really . . . nice."

Kristen stared at me, openmouthed, in the mirror. "He's *nice*?"

I turned my attention back to Kristen's long, layered hair. Yes, they were my friends, but I wasn't sure I felt comfortable talking about this. It was only two weeks ago that Kyle and I started hanging out just the two of us, talking more and kind of giving each other looks. Kyle was thoughtful and made me laugh. He was also brilliant at coming up with fun ideas for stuff to do, like when he took me hiking up Bended Brook, this steep, hilly trail that has a full view of our entire Massachusetts town. That ranks as one of the best things I've ever done in Rockford.

At the end of last weekend, I got the guts to ask him out. Just to get ice cream, no big deal—except that it *was* a big deal. We'd had a great time and when he dropped me off at home, he said we should do it again sometime. And that he would call me. Or text. I *think* it meant he was my boyfriend. But I still wasn't entirely sure. (How do you *know* when someone is your boyfriend? Is it like knowing when you've done well on a test or when you're having a really good hair day?)

Kristen and Lizbeth watched me closely, waiting for me to tell them more.

"Okay, he's more than nice," I finally admitted. "He's awesome."

"He is really sweet, Mickey," Lizbeth agreed.

"You guys!" Kristen said, clearly still not happy with the details—or lack thereof. "Mickey, at least tell us about your date last week. We still haven't heard about it. And have you had another date since that you haven't told us about? Or plans for another?"

"No," I said. "I mean, no other date. But, okay, last week," I said, figuring it wouldn't be horrible talking about something that had already happened. As opposed to talking about, you know, *my feelings*. "He met me at the salon after my shift and we walked to the Waffle Cone together. When we got there—"

"Did you guys hold hands on the way there?" Kristen interrupted.

"No, just wait," I said, starting to feel flustered again. I took a deep breath and pulled my special boar-bristle-and-nylon hairbrush, the very best kind on the market, through her hair. "So we got to the Waffle Cone—"

"You held hands later?" Kristen asked. "Because you haven't held hands all week at school."

"How would you know?" I asked her. Talk about feeling like I was under a microscope. Had she been watching me?

"Well, have you held hands?" Kristen pressed.

I sighed. "Yes. No. Look, do you want to hear the story or not?"

She clamped her hand over her mouth, her eyes gleaming, and nodded yes.

"Thank you," I said. "Okay, so we got there and he was totally sweet about getting us that table in the corner by the window, the one that's kind of private but you can see out onto Camden Way."

"Ooh, very nice," Lizbeth said.

"And then he, like, let me wait there while he went to get the ice cream. He totally wouldn't let me pay for it, even though I dug my money out of my wallet and practically threw it at him."

"Good." Kristen nodded as I twisted back her hair, thinking I might do some tousled bun look. "He should pay for it."

"You think?" I asked. "Even though I asked him out?"

"Of course," Kristen said. "He's the boy."

"That shouldn't matter," I said. "It's whoever does the asking out. Right, Lizbeth?"

She was looking at her phone, waiting for another message from Matthew, I guessed. "Hmm, I don't know. I kind of like the old-school idea of the guy paying, even though my mom says that in this day and age, a lady can pay her own way. It just seems more romantic."

"What's romantic about pulling money out of a wallet?" I asked.

Kristen said, "Do you really have to ask?"

I rolled my eyes.

"It's not about the money," Lizbeth said. "It's about taking care of things, even little stuff like ice cream. It's gentlemanly." Her phone buzzed, and when she looked down at the message she furrowed her brow. "Matthew just wrote, 'I'm your huckleberry.' What does that mean?"

"Like Huckleberry Finn?" I asked.

She shook her head in annoyance and dropped the phone back on the desk. "I have no idea. But I do think it was sweet of Kyle to pay. I really like him."

"He's really cool," Kristen agreed.

He *was* sweet and cool. He made me laugh and feel jittery, in a good way—like when he teasingly bumped my shoulder as we walked down the halls or called me after dinner to see how much progress I'd made on my homework.

"She's got that look on her face again," Kristen said, shaking her head as she eyed me in the mirror. I pinned her hair into a bun, then used the sharp end of the comb I'd brought to pull a few pieces out so it looked casual and effortless.

"Do we have that look on our faces when we talk about our boys?" Lizbeth asked Kristen. "Matthew did just tell me he was my huckleberry."

"But what does that mean?" I laughed.

Kristen and Lizbeth had been after Tobias and Matthew forever and somewhere in the last week had made it official. They were each a couple now, Kristen with Tobias and Lizbeth with Matthew. There wasn't any big declaration of them being together or the boys asking them to be their girlfriends. It just was. That's why I wondered about Kyle—did he think it *just was* for us, too? Can you be official if one person knows and one doesn't?

"Remember when they had the decency to be shy around us?" Kristen said. "Now I swear Tobias is on the verge of letting one rip in my presence. And when some guy starts telling you he's your huckleberry, sense needs to be knocked into him." She looked at Lizbeth in the mirror. "Remember how it felt the first time Matthew called you?"

"I thought I was going to have a heart attack," Lizbeth said. "But in a good way."

"And now?" Kristen asked.

Lizbeth thought for a moment, looking down at her phone. "Now I just wish he'd say things that make sense."

"See!" Kristen said. "The magic is already gone."

Lizbeth laughed. "You're being dramatic."

"No, I'm not," Kristen said. "I remember the first time Tobias asked me to go watch one of his baseball games. He was all nervous and could hardly look me in the eye. Now it's like he *expects* me to go to all his games. And he has like four a week. Mickey," she said to me, "trust me: You're in the good stages of your relationship with Kyle. Now it's your job to keep it there. Because believe me—he won't do it for you."

I noticed Lizbeth looking longingly at her phone. "Maybe *huckleberry* is code for something really endearing," she said. "Like calling someone cupcake or sweetie pie or something . . ."

I undid Kristen's hair and shook it out with my fingers. I divided it into two sections like pigtails and began twisting them toward her scalp. Then I tied it into a knot, securing it with an elastic.

"The time is *now*," Kristen said, staring intently into her own eyes in the mirror. "The dance is on Friday, girls. *Friday*. And none of our guys have even asked us yet."

"Kyle hasn't said anything to you?" Lizbeth asked me.

"Nope," I said. *Should he have?* I wondered. Had Jonah asked Eve?

"If we can't get Tobias and Matthew to ask us by Wednesday, then it's over," Kristen declared. "And that's cutting it close as it is. Right, Lizbeth?"

"I don't know," she said, bending the edge of the magazine cover. "I don't want to give Matthew some ultimatum."

"You're not," Kristen said. "You're just saying he needs to step it up. He's supposed to be your boyfriend."

"He is," Lizbeth said. "And I think he's a good boyfriend. You're the one with the problem with Tobias."

"Can't you just ask Tobias to the dance yourself?" I asked Kristen. I figured since they were officially boyfriend/girlfriend and they both knew it (unlike me and Kyle), then it wasn't a big deal.

Kristen raised her chin slightly and said, "I *can*. I just don't think I should have to."

"I bet Lizbeth can ask Matthew," I said, looking over

at her. "Right, Lizbeth?"

"I could mention it to him," she said. "But I'm positive he'll ask on his own. Just like I'm sure Kyle will ask Mickey."

"Or she could ask him herself." Kristen smiled. "Right, Mickey?"

I thought about when I asked Kyle out for ice cream. It was totally nerve-racking. Standing face-to-face with the person you liked and possibly being rejected was panic-inducing, to say the least. I had lived to tell it but I wasn't sure I wanted to do it again so soon.

"I mean, I could ask him," I said. "But I'm not really worried about it. I've actually barely thought about the dance. It's this Friday?"

"Oh, please," Kristen said.

Even Lizbeth laughed. "Yeah, Mickey. You're not fooling us."

"Step it up, Mick," Kristen said. "You and Kyle are just a couple of weeks behind me, Tobias, L, and Matthew. Crank up the volume on that relationship and we can all go through this stuff together."

I paused, avoiding Kristen's eyes looking back at me in the mirror. I felt dumb about asking this next question. Eve would know the answer and not think I was being silly at all. I really missed her. But I needed to know now, so Lizbeth and Kristen would have to do. "I just . . . I don't know. I mean—is he my boyfriend?"

"Duh!" Kristen said. "That's what we've been talking about!"

"But *we* never talked about it," I said. "Me and Kyle. Should I *assume* we're together?"

"That's a good point," Lizbeth said. "One date and hanging out at school a little more doesn't really mean he's your boyfriend. Does he walk you to your classes?"

"Sometimes," I said. "When we kind of run into each other in the halls."

"I think he's your boyfriend," Kristen said as if she refused to consider an alternative.

"You should talk to him about it, just to make sure," Lizbeth said.

I was more confused than ever. Was he my boyfriend? Were we going to the dance? Did he like me all that much, anyway? Would I have to ask him?

After a moment, Lizbeth asked, "Do you know if Eve and Jonah are going?"

For the slightest beat I paused. The mere mention of Eve's name made my stomach drop to the floor.

"I don't know," I said quietly.

"How are things going between you two, anyway?" Kristen asked. "Are you talking?"

"Not really. A little but . . . hardly at all."

"Oh, Mickey, I'm so sorry," Lizbeth said. "It'll get better."

"Yeah," Kristen said. "She'll come around. She just needs time."

"I know," I said, even though I wasn't sure.

"Has Jonah said anything about it?" Lizbeth asked.

"He's a boy," I answered.

"True," Kristen said. "But he's also your best friend."

"I know," I muttered.

"Maybe you should talk to him about it," Lizbeth said. "I know Eve needs time, but don't let too much go by. That'll only make things worse."

I hadn't thought of that, but Lizbeth was right. I'd already tried dipping my toe back into our friendship and that had gone nowhere. But if I waited too long, Eve might get used to not talking to me. That was something I really didn't want. I was surprised at how much I missed her after only a week, but I did miss her—and I needed her, too. She was the most levelheaded one of us. She'd know what I should do about Kyle. But if she needed a little space, the question was, how much space from me did she need?

CHAPTER 2

"Mickey, let's go! Doors opening in five," Mom said, poking her head out from her office.

I could hear a little bit of panic in her voice. Sunday mornings at the salon were always hectic. Mom liked us to be ready and waiting for our customers the moment they stepped inside.

"Coming!" I called as I inspected myself one last time in the mirror in the back room. I fluffed my long, curly hair, pulling it over my shoulders just so, and dabbed on a bit of lip gloss. Then I picked up my work apron, which I had carefully ironed that morning. I held it up for a moment and admired it.

There used to be exactly one thing I didn't like about my job as a sweeper at my mom's hair salon, Hello, Gorgeous!: I had to wear a black, plastic smock as my uniform. That was before Mom was featured on the show *Cecilia's Best Tressed*, where legendary hair stylist Cecilia von Tressell goes to salons around the country and takes them from good to outstanding. One of the outstanding things she did was throw out my degrading plastic smock and replace it with an adorable, dark-pink apron with ruffles around the edges and the Hello, Gorgeous! logo across the front pocket.

The other thing Cecilia did for the salon? Cranked up the volume on business.

"Mickey, we need more towels up here!" Devon, one of the stylists, called.

"Okay, I'll bring them."

"Mickey!" said Karen, the manicurist, from the bottom of the stairs to The Underground. "Bring me some cotton swabs, please? The extra-long ones."

"You got it!" I called down.

It had been like this all week. I used to say the salon was always busy, but that was nothing compared to how things were now. It was especially crazy considering the episode hadn't even aired yet. I guessed that all the business came from word of mouth around town that Cecilia von Tressell had given Hello, Gorgeous! a makeover. The phones hadn't stopped ringing since.

I stacked the towels next to the sinks, then dashed back for the cotton swabs and carried them downstairs into The Underground. What was once a horror-film setting with dust- (and bug-) covered floors, forgotten supplies, and rusted sinks was now all elegance and serenity. The walls were the color of vanilla-bean ice cream with a cream-and-black damask wallpaper on the back wall, a silver-and-crystal chandelier hung in the center, and more salon services than we'd ever offered, like private massage and waxing rooms and an expanded mani/pedi station were located there. Hello, Gorgeous! was finally the full-service salon it was always meant to be, all thanks to yours truly. If I hadn't texted Hello, Gorgeous! in to the show, Cecilia never would have come to Rockford.

I dashed downstairs to Karen's station. "Here you go," I said, handing the extra-long cotton sticks to her. Today she wore black tights and a baggy scoop-neck blouse that made her long neck look even more elegant than usual.

"Thanks, Mickey," she said. "I usually have a lot of walk-ins on Sunday, but today my schedule is half-booked. Pretty soon we're going to have to hire Cynthia full time." Cynthia occasionally helped Karen out, but lately her hours were getting longer and longer.

Upstairs, Mom was just opening the doors and the first clients of the day were walking in. Soon there'd be lots of chattering, hair dryers blowing, water splashing in sinks, and me, racing to keep up with it all.

That afternoon, Giancarlo, who happened to be my favorite person at the salon (aside from Mom, of course), was at his station working on a twenty-something woman who was getting deep-red extensions added to her shoulder-length hair. I knew extensions could take hours and this was a long, tedious process. I swept over to his station with my broom. (By the way, that's my official job—sweeper.)

"Get over here," he said as he worked his hands through the woman's hair. "Tell us what's happening while I show you the perfect way to braid in extensions."

"Nothing's happening," I said with a shrug. But I really wanted to talk about one thing—one *boy*—in particular, and Giancarlo was a great listener.

"Lies," he said. He turned to his client. "Jordana, this girl has a bona fide boyfriend now, and she claims that *nothing* is happening. Please."

I tried not to grin—especially at his outfit. Giancarlo was nothing if not outlandish in look and attitude. Today he wore white pants and a short, black cape. Seriously. A cape. I was impressed that he could pull it off. "You look extra fancy today," I said.

"Didn't you hear?" said Jordana. "He's extra *famous* today."

"Oh, hush," Giancarlo told her, with a huge grin on his face, which really meant that she should go on. "It's just a tiny little blog thing."

"What blog thing?" I asked.

"A little write-up on the *Berkshires Beauty* blog," he said, holding his head up a little higher. "They were here for Cecilia's visit, but apparently I styled the anonymous blogger herself."

"And she raved about it," Jordana said.

Giancarlo shrugged, but I knew he'd have taken a little bow if he weren't all tied up in his client's hair. "Just a few words of praise. One hundred and fifty-four, to be exact."

"Wow," I said. *Berkshires Beauty* was a big deal. "Congratulations."

"Thanks, honey," he said. "But we can talk about that later. I want to hear about you. What's happening in Mickeyland?"

I swept the pile of hair I had accumulated into a tight, little mound. "Well," I began. "There is something."

"Thought so," Giancarlo said, eyeing me.

"And it does have to do with a boy. The one I went out with last weekend."

"Of course it does. Kyle, right?"

I nodded.

"So spill it already."

I pushed my broom around the spotless floor, remembering everything the girls had said last night and all the things I felt about Kyle. "Well," I began. "He's nice. I really like him. It's just that . . ."

Giancarlo raised a brow. "Just that what?"

"Well, I don't know if he's, like, my boyfriend. Or just a boy friend."

Giancarlo paused, picking up a length of hair from his cart. "Of course he's your boyfriend," he said, looking at me.

"But how do I know?" I said, thinking about all the things Kristen and Lizbeth had said—who should pay for what, who should ask who to the dance. There seemed to be a lot of rules. "What if in his mind we're just hanging out? I haven't called him my boyfriend." I cringed just saying that out loud. "What if I called him that to his face and he was all, 'Uh, I don't think so'? That would be humiliating. For all I know he's texting some other girl right now."

"Mickey, honey, it's not like you have to have a formal discussion and shake on the matter," Giancarlo said. "Sometimes you just know when someone is your boyfriend. You hang around enough at school, then outside of school, then suddenly you're going out alone without your other friends, texting, and calling each other. And then, that's when you know. That's how it happens—little gradual moments like that." He brushed Jordana's increasingly long hair.

"That's not exactly how Kristen handles her relationship with Tobias," I said. "She basically tells him what he needs to do. Then they have a big fight, and then he does it."

Giancarlo laughed. "Look. Every relationship is different. You just have to figure yours out as you go along. And Kyle seems like he'd be a very good and understanding boyfriend."

Maybe he was right—both about Kyle being understanding and being my boyfriend. Which also meant that maybe I was someone's girlfriend. I thought about that for a moment. It felt very adult and official and scary. What was expected of me as a girlfriend? Did I have to start dressing up more? Play video games less? I wasn't sure I wanted to do either. I thought of Eve and Jonah and how, even though they spent a lot of time together, they were still pretty much themselves.

"There's something else," I said, shifting my broom in my hand and giving Giancarlo a steady look. "There's a dance on Friday."

"Ooh, fantastic," Giancarlo said. "School dances are the best. I remember my first one." He paused and gazed out the front window. "I took Bernadette

Milstein. I even helped pick out her dress and styled her hair."

I smiled, picturing Giancarlo as a teenager, helping his date get ready.

"My question is, are we automatically going together?" I asked. "Is it just assumed?"

"I'd bet my scissors you're going," Giancarlo said. "And you know what else? I have a fantastic idea. You must get your hair done here for the dance! How about you get your mom to give you a blowout. And send your gorgeous friend Eve to me, and I'll give her a wild, curled look. You two can switch styles for the night!"

My stomach dropped at the mention of Eve. Giancarlo still didn't know about our sort-of breakup. And now I didn't have the heart to tell him. I didn't want him to think less of me for what I'd done.

"Anyway," I said, changing the subject so we didn't have to talk about Eve, "I already asked Kyle out once," I said. "Do I have to do everything?"

"Don't stress so much," Giancarlo said. "Just talk to the boy. We're really not that scary."

"I know," I said. I'd never been scared to talk to Kyle before, but now that he was my probably-boyfriend, for some reason I was nervous.

As Giancarlo continued with Jordana's hair, I asked him, "You really think I'd look good with a total blowout? Like, straight hair, no curls?" I'd tried to straighten my hair once on my own to disastrous results.

"Girl, you could wear any style brilliantly," he said.

Okay, now do you see why Giancarlo is my favorite person at the salon? With flattery like that, who could argue?

I let Giancarlo focus on Jordana's hair so I could do a sweep of the salon. I felt better about things with Kyle. Giancarlo was probably right—we were, in fact, an item, even if there hadn't been some big proclamation.

After dumping my pile in a trash can in the back, I went up front to help Megan at reception. Mom was inspecting the new product wall—courtesy of Cecilia—but as I got closer I realized something was off about her. She wasn't wearing the crisp cotton suit she'd put on that morning. When would she have changed? And why? Something else was strange about her, too—the way she carried herself and how she inspected the wall as if she'd never seen it before. It wasn't until I tapped her shoulder and she turned to face me that I realized—this wasn't Mom at all.

CHAPTER 3

"Oh, I'm sorry," I said as the woman turned to me.

"It's okay," she said.

"Has someone helped you?" I asked, noticing that Megan had stepped away from the desk.

"No, not yet," she said. She looked me up and down and said, "What an adorable apron!"

The way to my heart! If I were the kind of person to say *I told ya so* to my mother, I totally would have done it right then. Instead I said, "Thank you. It's new."

"Well, it's fabulous," the woman said. "Most salons make their assistants wear these horrible plastic smock things. This looks much more professional."

"I know!" I said. She was so right!

"I'm Ana," she said. "What's your name?"

"Mickey," I said.

She held a bottle in her hands, one of the new

products Cecilia had brought in. It was a shine serum that helped make hair look radiant. "Did you know that cold water actually helps make hair shinier?" She winked and said, "Just a little trick from me to you."

She put the bottle back on the shelf, then folded her arms across her slim body. She looked out at the salon, taking it all in. "This place is cute. Looks like you do good business."

"Yes, we do," I said. "It's the best salon in town."

"I've heard about it," she said. "But I haven't had a chance to come in until now. You're getting lots of buzz, you know."

"Did you read about us on *Berkshires Beauty*?" I asked.

"That, among other places."

Wow, I thought. We really were getting famous! "So, do you have an appointment?" I stepped behind Megan's desk and looked at the monitor.

"Well, not yet. I wanted to stop in to make one." She looked across the salon. Her eyes immediately focused on one stylist in particular. "That must be the famous Giancarlo."

I looked back at him still working on Jordana's extensions and smiled. "The one and only," I said.

"I've been hearing his name around the salon community for years now," Ana said. "And then

Berkshires Beauty mentioned him specifically and said he gave her a fabulous color job. After that I knew I had to make the trip here to see him. And look at what great style he has!"

We both stood quietly and admired Giancarlo's cape.

"We all love him here. He's the best stylist," I said, beaming with pride. "Well, next to my mom, that is."

"Your mom? Is that Chloe Wilson?"

"Yes. How'd you know?" I asked.

She waved her hand like it was a lucky guess. "I just assumed the only person who could be better than Giancarlo is the owner. And she *is* the owner, right?"

"Yep. She's had the salon since I was six."

Ana smiled. "How sweet. And now you get to work here! I love that it's a family affair. Well," she said stepping closer to the reception desk, "if Giancarlo has any openings, I'd love to make an appointment for a color touch-up."

I turned back to look for Megan and saw that she was on her way up front. Good thing, because I wasn't allowed to use the reservation program on the computer. Cecilia had upgraded the system so we could book clients' appointments by phone, e-mail, and text message. Mom decided that she and Megan should be the only ones to access all that personal information.

"I'm here!" Megan said, her long hair flowing off

her shoulders. "I had to run to The Underground. Hi! How can I help you?"

"She needs to make an appointment with Giancarlo for a touch-up," I said. I looked back to Ana. "Megan will take care of you. It was nice talking to you."

"Nice talking to you, too, Mickey," she said. "And remember our little secret." She pointed to the fancy shine serums with a wink.

I grinned and nodded. This woman was more like my mom than anyone I'd ever met—perfectly put together with plenty of style tricks and tips up her tailored sleeve.

"Now!" Megan said as she looked at her computer. "Let's see when Giancarlo can fit you in. Do you prefer mornings or afternoons . . ."

As Megan took over, I happily went back to work. Giancarlo finished up Jordana's hair, and she left looking like a red bombshell.

I got back to sweeping and then had to attend to a minor emergency when a client accidentally knocked over the sanitizer at Devon's station. Later, Violet asked me to help clean up the foils on her station after a color job and Megan had me restock some products at the front.

At the end of the day, Mom found me while I gathered up hand towels from Karen's manicure station downstairs. She clicked over to me in her skinny heels and tailored skirt. And of course, her hair was perfect—never a strand out of place, a colored root showing, or a split end in sight. Today, her long, black hair hung loose down her back, the sides tucked neatly behind her ears.

"I'm about done," I said, ready to take the towels to the bin upstairs. I always went home before closing because Mom wanted to make sure I had plenty of time to do my homework.

"Need some help with that?" she asked, her rich-green eyes on the pile in my arms.

"I got it," I assured her.

A faint smile crossed her face. "Look at you. It's like you've worked here your whole life."

Mom looked at me with something like pride in her eyes. I felt relieved knowing I may have finally settled into working at the salon. It had certainly not been the easiest thing to do. But it was the only job I'd ever wanted—I couldn't wait to be a real stylist someday.

"Thanks, Mom," I said.

"Dad is making sandwiches for dinner," she said. "Can you stop at Farm Fresh on your way home and get some bread and cheese? He has turkey breast at home but needs a loaf of sourdough French and some Jarlsberg."

The thing about my dad—he loves food. *Good* food. So even though he claimed we were just having sandwiches, they'd be amazing sandwiches. The freshest and best-quality ingredients made with extra TLC.

"Yeah, sure," I said.

"Grab some money out of my wallet in my office. And great job today, as always."

Wow, I thought as I brought the towels upstairs. Mom hardly ever praised me. Not because she was mean or didn't think I did a good job, but she's a perfectionist and I had blown it at the salon on one or two (or seventeen) occasions. So when she told me I'd done a great job—*as always*—I felt like I'd just been accepted into the most prestigious salon training in the world. Like I was finally *in.*

After I hung up my apron and grabbed some money, I walked to Farm Fresh, which doubled as a little café with a few round tables in the back. They served the best grilled cheese sandwiches in the world. I'm talking ooey-gooey wonderfulness made with fancy cheeses like Gruyère, Manchego, and Gouda. I got in line and ordered a half pound of their Jarlsberg, per Mom's orders. Then I stood back to wait as my order was filled. I wondered if there was anything in the world more decadent than a good grilled cheese sandwich. Doubtful.

I gazed into the small dining area, thinking I should ask Mom and Dad if we could come here for dinner more often, when I saw something that made me catch my breath. It was Eve, sitting with another girl, laughing and eating one of those ooey-gooey grilled cheeses. The girl pulled a string of cheese off her chin, then wiped it on Eve's plate. Eve laughed and swatted her hand away.

I'd never seen this girl before and wondered who she was. Had Eve already found someone to replace me? I didn't like the looks of what I saw, and no, it was not because I was instantly jealous that Eve was having fun with someone besides me. It wasn't that at all (except maybe a little).

Since Eve moved to town a couple of months ago, I'd been one of her only friends, along with Kristen and Lizbeth. We'd clicked right away. She was nice with a slightly snarky attitude that made Jonah choke on his words. Who wouldn't love that quality in a friend?

I realized I was staring, possibly openmouthed. Eve turned toward me, her face bright with laughter, and before I could look away we locked eyes. She looked as stunned as I felt, and I quickly turned away. I stepped closer to the counter, willing the cheese guy to hurry up with my order. I glanced back to see if she was still looking at me—maybe she hadn't really seen me?—but when I did it was clear she was looking right at me. And she wasn't laughing anymore. I turned away again. I couldn't stand there in that tiny shop any longer.

I tried to act casual as I started for the door, not wanting to draw any attention to myself. Just as I reached it, though, a woman touched my arm. She pointed back to the counter and said, "You forgot your order."

I looked back and saw the cheese guy had just slapped down a white paper package on the counter.

"Thanks," I said, scrambling back to the counter. Out of the corner of my eye I saw Eve lean across the table to whisper something to her new friend. I snatched the package from the counter and bolted out the doors.

CHAPTER 4

"Blue cheese?"

Dad looked inside the wrapped paper I'd brought home from Farm Fresh with a disappointed expression on his face. "Did you tell her to get blue cheese?" he asked Mom, who was leaning on the kitchen island.

She shook her head. "Jarlsberg."

"That's blue cheese?" I asked Dad, leaning over to look.

"Yes." He sniffed it, then broke off a small piece and popped it in his mouth. "I mean, it's delicious and all, but maybe not the best choice for turkey sandwiches."

"Sorry, Dad," I said, sinking into a chair. "I must have grabbed the wrong package."

"Well. That's okay. We'll make due. Now where's that bread?"

"The bread."

Dad raised his brows at me. "Did you forget the bread?"

I sighed. "I'm sorry. I guess I spaced." Considering what had just happened with Eve, I was surprised I made it home.

"You okay?" Dad asked, his full attention on me now.

"I'm fine," I said, rubbing my eyes. "Just tired."

Mom came over and rubbed my back. "Tough day at the office?"

I faked a smile. "Something like that."

"Well," Dad said, looking around the kitchen. "We can still make this work. We've got a decent loaf in here somewhere, and maybe if I add bacon, or if we had pears . . ."

Dad rummaged through the refrigerator, and Mom gave me another look. "You sure you're okay? You look a little distracted," she said. "Everything all right at school?"

Dad dropped his new ingredients on the counter and closed the refrigerator door. "Want to tell us about it?"

"Well . . . ," I began. Dad started to chop the bacon while Mom went to the cabinet and took down some dinner plates. But I knew all their attention was on yours truly. "It's Eve."

"I thought you two weren't speaking?" Mom said

delicately. She and Dad knew about the problems we'd had. It wasn't just my intervening in her and Jonah's relationship, but there had also been a slight (major) mishap with coloring her hair, too.

"We're not," I said. "Like, definitely not."

"What does that mean?" Dad asked.

"Nothing," I said, suddenly not sure I wanted to talk about this. I mean, my parents were cool and all, but they weren't my friends. I wasn't sure I wanted to confide in them about this.

"We don't want to pressure you," Mom said gently. "But we're here if you want a little help."

"Or to just talk stuff out," Dad offered.

For some reason, that alone made me feel better, if just a tiny bit. "Well," I continued. "It's just, I saw her at Farm Fresh with some girl I don't know. And it looked like they were having a lot of fun."

Mom nodded like she understood. "Maybe it was a relative of hers. A cousin?" she suggested.

"Maybe," I said. I actually hadn't thought of that.

"She didn't introduce you?" Dad asked.

"We were sort of on opposite sides of the shop," I said, which of course drew looks from my parents. Farm Fresh was about as big as a walk-in closet.

"You didn't feel like you could go say hello?" Mom asked.

I shook my head no, remembering how terrified I'd

felt seeing her. "I just felt weird, I guess. The look she gave me was just . . . weird." I couldn't think of another word to describe it. Except maybe *awful*.

"I'm sure she feels the same way," Mom said. "And remember, a look can mean a thousand things—none of them what you might think. Don't jump to conclusions until you actually speak with her."

"I'm sure she'll come around," Dad said. "In the meantime, we're here if you need us."

This time, my forced smiled wasn't entirely fake. Not entirely real, either—but it was progress.

"If you want to know my opinion," Dad said, placing a pan on the stove, "I think there's nothing better at a time like this than a little comfort food. How about grilled blue cheese with diced bacon?"

"I think it sounds amazing," Mom said, a dash of extra enthusiasm in her voice.

Dad got back to fixing dinner as Mom came over to the table and sat across from me. "So what's new at the salon?" he asked, an obvious effort to change the subject.

"Well," Mom said, glancing at me with a grin. "The salon has been incredible, thanks very much for asking. Business is already up from this time last year and the *Best Tressed* episode hasn't even aired yet. That post in *Berkshires Beauty* has set the local salon industry buzzing. I'm sure they're all texting in, trying to get on Cecilia's show now that we've done it."

"We all knew doing *Cecilia's Best Tressed* was going to be amazing for the salon. Right, Mickey?" Dad teased, because that's not exactly how it went down. When Cecilia's cameras showed up at the salon unannounced, Mom had had one of her biggest meltdowns yet with all her energy and anger directed at yours truly. "Mickey, want to butter one side of each of these slices?"

From across the island, Dad passed a plate of bread, the butter, and a knife to me, and I started smearing.

"Yes, well," Mom began, "I'm not sure we *knew* anything. But it did turn out great."

I kept buttering the bread, only half paying attention to what I was doing. I tried to analyze the look on Eve's face at Farm Fresh even though Mom had said I shouldn't read into it. Why had she looked stunned? Why had her laughter faded? Was she trying to hide that new girl from me? Who was she, anyway?

"Maybe we should have a party when the episode premieres," Dad said.

"Maybe. But first I have to do my Head Honchos gig," Mom said, leaning back in her chair. The Head Honchos on Cecilia's show observed the salon's stylists and offered recommendations. Mom and everyone else had been pretty frustrated with them while they were in Hello, Gorgeous!, but now I guess she saw the value in them.

"Mickey," she said, looking at me. "You'll like this. They're providing hair and makeup for the filming. What do you think—should I let them do my hair? Think some television stylist can do a better job than I can?"

For once I wasn't excited about talking about the salon or hairstyles or Cecilia and her show. The only thing I seemed capable of thinking about was Eve and that look she gave me. Still, I managed to say, "Yeah, I think you should try it."

"Maybe," Mom said thoughtfully. "Or maybe you can style it for me." I knew she was only trying to cheer me up. For a brief moment I did think about styling Mom's hair. Then I pushed the thought out of my head. Talk about pressure.

"Mickey, I think that's enough butter, honey," Dad said.

I looked down at the plate in front of me. I'd slathered butter on the slices as if I were laying bricks. "Sorry, Dad," I said. Dad slid the plate away from me. He winked, which forced a smile on my face. With the smallest gesture, he could get me.

"Mickey," Mom began. "I've actually been wanting to talk to you all weekend."

Okay, nothing good ever came out of Mom

wanting to talk to me on the heels of talking about the salon. Never. Still, I turned to face her even though I had no idea what I'd done this time.

"The salon is doing outstanding," she began. "Everyone's been in such great spirits, the town has really rallied around us, and like I said, business is up. I have you to thank for all this. I know I was skeptical at first about the reality show, but I see now how much it's paying off. So I wanted to reward you."

"Really?" I asked, curious. Mom was so strict about her salon that I just assumed that anything good I did was *expected*. Like, I shouldn't expect a reward for something I was supposed to be doing already.

"I've spoken with Giancarlo," she continued, "and he's agreed to let you be his assistant for an afternoon or two, if you'd like. You'll just be doing basic stuff, like getting things he needs, but I thought you could also spend the time learning more about how he styles, how he got started—whatever questions you might have for him."

"Seriously?" I asked. I was shocked. This wasn't a little reward. This was huge! Mom knew I wanted to be a professional stylist, but I didn't think she'd let me do any training at her salon until high school, maybe. Now I wondered if Mom finally thought I had something real to bring to the salon, a know-how or talent. Like maybe all I needed was just a little more education and experience. That meant more to me than just about anything.

"I'm very proud of you," she said. "Just make sure you keep up your regular duties—okay?"

"Okay," I said. "I will." I smiled—my first real smile since seeing Eve at Farm Fresh.

Maybe things were looking up. Praise from Mom didn't come easily. And this was basically giving me an all-access pass to her salon and employees. I wondered if now was the time to push forward with Eve, too, and stop dancing around the real issue. Yes, I had messed up royally, but if she still wanted to be friends then we should be friends, right? A break didn't help that. I mean, what did she need space for if she wanted to still be friends? I decided I needed to talk to the only person I knew who might have the answer—my best friend, Jonah.

CHAPTER 5

"I didn't see you all weekend," Jonah said as we walked to school the next morning like we did most mornings. "What'd you do?"

"Not much," I said as I adjusted the top of my wide-neck, marigold blouse. "Just worked at the salon. Hung out with Kristen and Lizbeth on Saturday." *Without Eve,* I wanted to add, but I knew I had to ease him in. Boys. They never understood what we were saying, let alone not saying.

"Cool," he said.

"Yeah. I guess. It was kind of weird, though," I continued. When Jonah didn't say anything or even glance at me, I said, "You know, because Eve wasn't there Saturday night. I wonder how much longer she's going to be mad at me."

Hint, hint, nudge, nudge, shake him by the shoulders. Hey, he wasn't my best friend for nothing.

I was entitled to ask questions.

Jonah didn't say a word, just squinted into the sun through the trees, avoiding me entirely.

"Come on, Jonah. Has she said anything to you about me at all?"

Finally he shook his head. Communication! "No, she hasn't."

"Are you sure? Not one word? If she's said *anything,* you have to tell me," I pressed. There could be some meaning behind something she said that he wouldn't think anything of.

"She hasn't said a word, Mick. I swear."

"Nothing?" I asked, my mood deflating.

"Nothing," he said.

I didn't think it was possible but I felt worse knowing that she hadn't even asked or said anything about me. Like she wasn't even thinking about me or missing me.

"But honestly, we didn't talk much this weekend," he said, seeing how disappointed I was.

"Was she busy or something?" I asked. I wanted to know about her new friend, but knowing that she hadn't thought about me at all made me feel so bad I couldn't imagine that hearing about the other girl would help anything.

"We both had other plans. Kyle and I skated and went to the movies on Saturday and she was out with some friend on Sunday. That's all I know, I promise."

Some *friend*. There it was. She hadn't been with a cousin or a long-lost sister recently returned from an evil stepfather. (Okay, I know that was reaching.) Eve had a new friend. She'd moved on from me.

"Yeah, no—it's not a big deal," I said, trying not to sound desperate.

"Hey, you should come over tonight or something. I've got a new game that I know you'd kill on."

"Is Kyle coming over?"

"No," he said. "I meant just us. We haven't hung out in a long time."

He was right—it had been forever. Or, more specifically, since Eve became his girlfriend and Kyle became my . . . whatever he was. I still wasn't sure. Truthfully, I missed Jonah. I may be a girl who loves a good hairbrush, but I also go crazy for blowing up video game aliens.

"That'd be fun," I said, feeling a little better at his offer. "Let's do it."

"Okay," he said. "Better prepare yourself for a whopping."

"Please." I smiled. "So, you and Kyle hung out this weekend?"

"Yup," he said. And then, nothing.

I couldn't believe Jonah. Could he not give me anything?!

"Cool," I said, race cars doing laps in my stomach.

Had he asked about me? Confided in Jonah about me? Said *anything*? Was anyone in this town talking about me?!

"And in case you're wondering," Jonah said, turning his eyes to me, "*he* did ask about you."

"I wasn't wondering," I said quickly.

"Okay," he said with a grin. "Then you don't want to know what he said, I guess."

I know violence is never the answer but I punched him in the arm—lightly. "Jonah Goldman, you better tell me every word!"

He laughed. "Relax! He basically did what you just did. *'So, how's Mickey? Have you hung out with her lately?'* Man, I hope your conversations with each other are better. You two are boring me to death."

Our conversations were just fine, thank you very much, so I didn't care about Jonah's opinion on that particular subject—I was too busy trying to suppress the goofy smile pulling itself up on my face. Kyle had asked about me. Which meant that when he wasn't around me, he was thinking about me like I was thinking about him. I wonder what he thought.

As we walked toward school, I wondered if today would be the day Kyle asked me to the dance. Or I would ask him. Or we just assumed we'd go together? The dance was in five days and although Giancarlo had been helpful with lots of other things, he'd never given me a firm answer on this subject.

"Do you think he's going to ask me to the dance? I mean, did you guys talk about the dance at all?" I asked.

"Dances," Jonah sneered. "A favorite subject of dudes."

"Did you just call yourself a dude?"

He shifted his eyes to me and said, "We didn't talk about it."

Fine, I thought. I could wait to see what would happen. I was patient like that.

After being agonizingly patient all morning, Kyle caught up with me in the halls on my way into the caf. "Thank god it's Monday, right?" he teased as we fell in step with each other.

"Yeah," I said, rolling my eyes, acting like I was all cool, but truthfully my heart had picked up its pace. "My favorite day of the week."

As if his plan was to make my heart beat even faster than it already was, Kyle pushed his dark hair—with the softest, subtlest curls—off his forehead.

"Did you do anything fun this weekend?" he asked.

"Hung out with my friends," I said, not mentioning *friends minus one*. "Nothing too exciting. What about you?"

He shrugged. "About the same. Wow, we're really partiers, huh?"

I smiled. "Big-time."

"Got any tests this week?" he asked. I swear, every time he looked at me, I felt like he was seeing something that no one else saw. My heart went from racing to a near-dead stop. I was starting to sweat.

"No, thank goodness," I said, telling myself to be cool. "I swear they gave us all these intense projects three weeks in a row, and this week—nothing. Why can't the teachers get together and share what they're all doing so they don't pile it on us at once?"

"Totally agree," Kyle said. "Last week I had four tests, and three of them were on the same day. They should have, like, a chart or something in the teachers' lounge where they post their tests and projects due."

"Why can't teachers think logically like we do?"

He shook his head wearily and said, "It's a travesty."

We turned the corner that led to the cafeteria, and our hands brushed. I pulled my hand away, hoping he didn't think I was trying to get him to hold my hand(!!). He quickly glanced at me like maybe he thought I had, so I crossed my arms over my chest in a totally unnatural way. I could feel the sweat bubbling on my upper lip—super attractive, I know. I reached up casually and tried to wipe under my nose, then hoped he didn't think I was trying to *pick* my nose. I dropped my arms back down by my sides.

We walked beneath a huge banner that stretched wall to wall reading LET'S DANCE! FRIDAY AT 7.

Kyle looked up at the sign and said, "Um, so. I, uh . . ."

"Yes?" I replied.

"I like that top you're wearing," he said, glancing briefly at my top. He quickly averted his eyes. Did he just look at my boobs? Like there was anything there to see! I crossed my arms back again, just in case. "It's, um . . . I like the way the neck part is." He motioned to his own neck.

As embarrassed as I was, I thought how very sweet it was that he noticed my top. At the moment, it was better than any mention of the dance. Jonah wouldn't notice something I was wearing if it had speakers on it and announced, "I AM A PRETTY, MARIGOLD BLOUSE!"

"Thanks," I said. "You can borrow it anytime. Just let me know."

He grinned and a blush crept over his entire face as he said, "Ha-ha. Very funny."

"It'll look good on you! I think this particular shade of yellow is perfect for your coloring."

"Knock it off," he said, bumping my shoulder with his. I have to say that the bump was just as good as any hand-holding. At least for now.

In the cafeteria, Kristen and Lizbeth were sitting at our usual table waiting for everyone. They both looked exceptionally cute today—Kristen wore a dress with a tiny flower print, and Lizbeth had on a colorful silk scarf that she wore as a thick headband. They always looked good, but today I was a little suspicious.

"Hey, guys," I said as Kyle and I sat down next to each other instead of across from each other like we used to. More confirmation that he was more than just a friend, I guess.

"Hey, Mickey," Kristen said, biting into an orange slice and looking over at Tobias and Matthew's table.

Opening up my packed lunch, I asked the girls, "Something going on with you two?"

"Mickey," Lizbeth said, straightening her headband and glancing at the boys' table. "You should know by now that something is *always* going on with us."

Kyle and I grinned. "She's right," I said to him.

"And as usual," Kyle said, "I don't want to know."

Jonah finally came over to the table but Eve was nowhere in sight.

"Hey, man," he said to Kyle, leaning his hands on the table but not sitting down. He had a handful of napkins clutched in one hand. "We still on for after school?"

"Like Donkey Kong," Kyle said.

Sometimes it saddened me to know that I knew these video game references the boys made. Especially vintage video game references.

"Cool," Jonah said, pushing back from the table. "See you then."

"Uh, hello!" I said, stopping him before he bolted. "Can you not say hi to the rest of us?" I motioned to Kristen and Lizbeth, who hadn't even noticed him.

"Sorry," Jonah said. "Hey, Mickey."

"Where're you going? Where's Eve?"

"Er, we're, uh . . . we're actually in the hall studying for English. I just dropped by for some napkins."

"Really?" I said. Eve and I had the same English class. "Is there some test or project coming up?"

"No," Jonah said. He started tearing a little at the napkins. "Just, you know—general studying. So I better get back. See you guys later."

"See you after school, man," Kyle said as Jonah dashed out of the cafeteria like he was chasing someone who just stole his skateboard.

Wow, I thought. My mind filled with the image of Eve's face and the look she gave me at Farm Fresh. Then I remembered what Jonah had said on our walk to school—that Eve hadn't mentioned me at all.

I tried to pretend that this didn't mean anything—as if Jonah and Eve both just happened to not eat in the cafeteria on occasion. But the look Kyle was giving me—brows raised and crunched together like he was watching a commercial for the Humane Society—made me feel terrible all over again.

I sighed.

"You okay?" Kyle asked.

Kristen and Lizbeth looked over and it was clear they'd pulled their attention away from their boys long enough to check on me. "Yeah, Mick," Kristen said. "Are you okay? You look a little pale."

I nodded. I didn't want to bother them with this mess or jeopardize their friendships with Eve by dragging them into it. "It's nothing," I said.

"Bull," Lizbeth said.

"Yeah, bull," Kristen agreed. "Now spill it."

When I didn't say anything, Lizbeth said, "We know it's about Eve. You can tell us, Mickey."

"Fine," I said, glancing at Kyle. I guess I really did want to talk about it. "I saw Eve last night at Farm Fresh with some other girl. Someone I'd never seen before. I think Eve saw me, too, but she didn't even say hello. It was awkward times ten."

"Well," Lizbeth began, choosing her words carefully. "Maybe she didn't see you. Eve isn't the type to give the cold shoulder." I gestured to Eve's empty seat at the table. "Not when you're standing right in front of her, I mean. She's not petty like that."

"Yeah," Kristen agreed. "That's more of a move

I'd make."

I smiled the smallest smile, shaking my head at Kristen.

"I'm just saying," she said.

"Do you want us to talk to Eve for you?" Lizbeth asked. "Just to get things started?"

"Break the ice before we break that mystery girl's bones," Kristen said.

"Kristen!" Lizbeth said. "Give it a rest. Hey, do you have any idea who she was with?" she asked me.

"No clue," I said. "I even asked Jonah but he just said 'some friend.'"

"I'm sure she's no one," Kristen said.

"Yeah," Kyle agreed, chiming in. "And even if she is your new replacement, I doubt she's as cool as you."

I froze, staring down at my sandwich. He'd said it, my greatest fear. Being replaced. I picked up the sandwich and took a bite, but it felt like chewing on paper. I gnawed it around in my mouth, pretty sure I looked like a cow. Gross. If I cared any less I would have just spit it out.

"Hey, I'm sorry," Kyle said. He turned to face me, touching my arm briefly before pulling away. "That was an awful attempt at humor. I shouldn't have said that. It was stupid."

I forced the food down and said, "It's okay."

"No, it was dumb," he said. I glanced up and saw Kristen and Lizbeth pretending not to watch but totally watching. "Seriously, I'm sorry. Okay?"

I looked at Kyle, whose brown eyes showed how he truly felt—worried and sorry. He looked so eager for me to forgive him that I couldn't help giving him a half smile. "Mr. Smooth."

He smiled back, and this time when he touched my arm, just above my elbow, he left his hand there for one assured moment, giving me a little squeeze.

"Oh my gosh," Lizbeth said suddenly, breaking into our moment. I turned to see what she and Kristen were looking at. Tobias and Matthew were eyeing the girls from their table. "This could be it."

Kyle dropped his hand, and we both looked at my friends. "It, what?" he asked.

"The dance!" Kristen said as if everyone should know the answer. "You are aware that there is a dance at the end of this week, aren't you? We're going to give them a chance to ask us before we ask them."

"Come on, Kristen," Lizbeth said, standing up slowly. Kristen stood as well. "They're motioning us over. Mickey, if you want, we'll do some digging, find out who that girl Eve's hanging out with is."

"Yeah," Kristen said. "And we'll hate her if you want us to."

"I don't want you to hate her," I said. "I don't even know her."

"You know what I mean. Okay, we gotta go," Kristen said, her eyes focused on the guys.

"I'll see you later," I said.

Once Kyle and I were alone, I wondered if the subject of the dance would come up. I kind of hoped it would and he would just ask me, or confirm that we were going together, or do whatever it was that was supposed to happen.

"So," Kyle began, breaking the silence. "Are they a little more . . . excited than usual? It's just a school dance, right?"

"Yeah, just a dance," I said. "But you know Kristen and Lizbeth. They don't need much of a reason to get . . . excited." I smiled at Kyle's care with his words when talking about my friends. I wouldn't be surprised if he flat out called them crazy man-eaters, but I did appreciate that he didn't.

I waited for Kyle to say more about the dance but he didn't. As we finished up, I wondered what he'd meant when he said, "It's just a school dance." Did that mean he didn't want to go? Or that he didn't know if I'd want to go? I sighed again. It was only Monday and I already wished the subject of our spring dance would go away.

CHAPTER 6

On my way out of school that afternoon I spotted Eve standing to the side of the front steps, staring at the street where parents parked, waiting to pick up their kids.

Eve had kept up her polite ignoring of me through our English class, which is right after lunch. That's how it seemed, anyway. Between the look, the not coming to lunch, and the not saying hi in class, I figured it was a pretty safe guess. I reminded myself that even though I understood her wanting to take a step back from our friendship, I didn't want her to step so far back that we were no longer friends. So I took a deep breath, ignored the voice in my head that told me to run the other way, and walked toward her.

"Hey, Eve," I said. "Waiting for your mom?"

She flicked her eyes at me, then looked away as if she were startled to see me. "No, my mom is at my grandma's today," she said.

She didn't explain any further. I hated the awkwardness between us, but at least she had said something to me.

Finally, she looked at me again. "Hey, can I ask you something?"

"Yeah, sure," I said, trying not to sound too eager but really wanting to scream, "YES!" I hoped she'd ask about the dance or maybe tell me she *thought* it was me yesterday but wasn't sure and she was sorry if she came off as rude.

She put her hands in her pockets and asked, "Do you have to do an invention project for your science class?"

"I—" *What? Just school stuff?* "No," I said, deflated. "Why?"

"I have Ms. Howard," she said. "And get this—we have to come up with an invention by Friday."

"That's rough," I said. It may not have been best-friend conversation, but she was talking to me. In a casual, normal, friend kind of way. It was better than nothing.

"I know. Like she thinks we're all Einsteins or something. Or Thomas Edisons . . . or whoever invented a lot of stuff."

I smiled. "I think they were both pretty smart."

"Well, see what I mean? I don't even know who

the great American inventor is and I'm supposed to come up with my own invention by Friday? Is she kidding?"

"That does seem kind of fast," I said, because it did. "Maybe you can do something like, um . . . you could invent a way to keep your cereal from getting soggy in the morning. You know how once you pour the milk you're, like, committed to eating the cereal in less than two minutes? If there were some drops or a cream or something that you could add, then you could let your cereal sit for hours before eating!"

Eve stared at me for a moment, clearly unable to answer. Perhaps it was because I had just suggested something insane. What was I thinking? I was just so eager to be helpful—eager, or maybe desperate. Take your pick.

"Thanks," she said slowly. "That seems pretty complicated and like something I'd have to get approved by, like, the FDA or something."

"Right," I said. "Of course." Because duh.

"This just seems like something that should be for a college graduation project or something. Don't you think?"

"Totally," I said. "I once had to do this project on the founding fathers, and I completely forgot it was due until—"

"Hey, guys." We heard a voice coming up to us.

We turned and I saw the girl from Farm Fresh strolling up the lawn, a straw fedora covering her short, shaggy hair. "What's up?" She looked me up and down like she was inspecting every inch of me. She wore a pale-yellow mesh top with a white tank beneath.

She had cute style, even though I didn't want to admit it. Who was she? This friend-stealing, style-savvy girl?

"Hey, Marla," Eve said to her. "Glad you found your way over here okay. She walked here from my house on her own," Eve explained to me.

I wanted to say, *Big deal. It's like four blocks.* I also wanted to say, *And who are* you? but I managed to keep my mouth shut. Clearly I was feeling defensive.

"She's visiting her cousins for the week. And me, of course," Eve said.

The girl—Marla—looked from me to Eve and back again. She was probably wondering what I was wondering—did Eve plan on introducing us?

As awkwardness built, she finally gave me a little wave and a smile and said, "Hello."

"Oh my gosh, I'm so rude!" Eve said, snapping to. "Mickey, this is my friend Marla from Ridgeley."

"Hi," I said, smiling.

"Marla, this is Mickey," Eve said.

Marla's smile faltered. "Mickey?" she said. She turned to Eve. "*The* Mickey—"

"So!" Eve said, cutting her off and brightening up a

bit too much. I felt sick to my stomach. What had Eve told her?

"You're from Ridgeley?" I said, even though Eve had just said it. My mind was racing—Eve hadn't introduced me as her friend like she had for Marla. She'd just said Mickey.

"Yes," she replied. "Eve and I were best friends until she ditched us for this place."

This place?

"Marla's spring break is later than ours," Eve explained. "She has the week off and some of her family is close by so she's spending the days with them and the evenings with me. Worked out perfectly."

"That's cool," I said. Sure, everything was perfect for them. All I wanted was to get away. I had to be nice, though, even if Marla was looking at me like she wanted to shove me. "I was actually just about to invite Eve to the Waffle Cone." Lie, but not the point. "You have not experienced Rockford until you've had one of their signature ice creams in a homemade cone. You'll never buy ice cream at the grocery store again. What do you say?"

No one said anything at first. Marla gave Eve this look that I couldn't read—a tiny smile and raised eyebrows. Did that mean *Let's go!* Or was it more, *Seriously? This girl is desperate and crazy and so not worth your time.*

"That sounds really fun," Eve finally said. "But I promised to take Marla to the old cemetery. We're going to see what the oldest tombstone there is."

"Oh, okay. Have fun," I said, thinking maybe they would ask me to come along. Eve was thoughtful like that. She would totally do it.

"Thanks, though," Eve said.

"Yeah, thanks," Marla said. "You ready, Eve?"

At least I could finally say I knew what it felt like to be rejected to your face. It felt a lot like being kicked in the stomach. Could I really blame them, though? Marla was in town to spend time with Eve, not some pseudofriend of Eve's. And not even a *good* pseudofriend. A pretty lousy one.

"See you at school tomorrow," Eve said.

"I heard there's a tombstone from the 1600s there," I called as they walked away. "Keep an eye out!"

Marla smiled and looked back at me, and then I swore I heard her say, "I thought you weren't friends with her . . ."

But they were sort of far away by then. It's hard to say for sure. I probably didn't hear her right . . .

CHAPTER 7

"You're terrible!" Jonah said.

"Give me five more minutes and I'll overtake your position," I said.

We were at Jonah's playing a new Enemy Warcraft game he'd picked up over the weekend. There were tanks, machine guns, snipers, hostages—the works. But since I'd never played this version before, I needed a couple of rounds to settle in.

It'd been a while since we'd hung out together, just the two of us, like old times. It felt really good and easy, like no time had passed at all.

"Ka-blewy!" Jonah yelled as he demolished my position in the bushes.

I tossed the remote in mock anger and said, "How can you possibly be satisfied knowing you beat me at a game I've never played before?"

"Because," he said with a smile, "I know the next

time we play you'll kill me."

"Probably," I said.

"Want to go another round?" he asked.

"You got it."

This time, I understood the game better and beat him. Not by much, but still—I won.

Before I went home for dinner, I told Jonah, "We should hang out more, just us. If your ego can stand it, that is."

"It is pretty hard being friends with someone who constantly whops you," he said. "But yeah, you're right. We should hang out more."

As I walked to the back door I said, "See you in the morning?"

"Yep," he said. "Breakfast at your place."

At least some things didn't change.

After dinner, I helped Mom clear the dishes and put away the tiny bit of leftover grilled chicken and asparagus. She and Dad went upstairs to watch TV in their room and I settled in at the table to do homework. I was totally into the algebra worksheet (ha-ha, not) when there was a knock at the back door.

"Come in!" I said, figuring it was Jonah. No one else knocked on or came through that door but him. Our backyards backed up to each other and there was a gate built into our fences. He came through it most mornings, stopping in our kitchen for breakfast before we walked to school together.

The door slowly opened, and around the frame popped an unexpected, unsure face: Kyle's.

"Hey!" I said, standing up.

"Hey," he said, staying behind the door. "Is it okay to come in?"

"Of course," I said. "I thought you were Jonah."

Kyle stepped inside and shut the door behind him. "He told me I could come in this way. I hope that's okay."

"It's fine," I said. "Wanna sit down?"

"No, that's okay. I was actually wondering if you wanted to go for a walk?" he asked. Except it was kind of like he asked the kitchen table, not me. He only flicked his eyes up to meet mine after he asked the question.

"Yeah, sure," I said. "Let me just go tell my parents."

I flew up the stairs and asked if I could go out with Kyle.

I should have known it wouldn't be that easy. There was a boy, in our house, asking me to go for a walk at dusk on a Monday.

"Hello there," Dad said, following me back into the kitchen. He held out his hand. I was mortified. Fully and completely mortified at what was about to happen.

I looked to Kyle, whose eyes had gone a bit buggy, his shoulders inching up toward his ears.

"Hello, sir," Kyle said.

Sir?!

"Kyle, is it?" Dad asked, even though he knew because I told him five seconds ago.

"Yes, sir. Kyle Lancaster."

"Where are you kids heading off to on a school night?" he asked.

"Dad," I said, my back slumping in annoyance. "I told you, we're just going for a walk. I'll be back in fifteen minutes."

"Kyle, son," he said, ignoring me. "What are your plans for the future?"

"Dad!"

"College? Work?" he continued as Kyle stood stunned, his mouth slightly agape. "Military?"

"We're going," I said. I knew Dad was joking but Kyle didn't, which was all that mattered. "I'll be back in fifteen."

Dad finally smiled and pulled me into a side hug. He kissed my head—mortification overload!—and said, "Make it twenty."

That was why I tolerated the old man.

Outside, we started in the direction of Camden Way, the main street in town, and also where Hello, Gorgeous! was located. Before we got too far, Kyle said, "Why don't we turn off here and go to the park?"

"Okay," I said. The park was a huge open area with picnic tables, a playground, and benches, and on the other side near the woods was the start of some hiking trails. Since it was after dinnertime and the sun was starting to set, not too many people were still out. "Sorry about my dad. I think he was more interested in embarrassing me than grilling you."

"Yeah, no biggie," Kyle said, but judging by how quickly he responded, I didn't quite believe him. I didn't think my dad could be that intimidating, but then again I wasn't a boy meeting him for the first time.

We walked a little farther in silence, listening to evening sounds—low rumbles of the occasional car in the distance, some kids yelling at a ball game, crickets chirping.

"Do you have any homework tonight?" Kyle asked.

"A little math," I said. "Do you?"

He shoved his hands in his jeans pocket and said, "Some history, but I finished it at Jonah's."

"Is that what happens at the late shift over at Jonah's? Homework?" I asked. "I'm impressed."

"We did a worksheet together so we could play video games." He looked at me sideways and said, "His mom made us."

"Should have known." I laughed. "So I guess he

practiced with me before he creamed you. What'd you guys play?"

"Enemy Warcraft."

"And who won?"

"Jonah," Kyle said, grinning. "He killed me."

We came up to a bench and sat down, looking out at the empty, green lawn while the sun started to dip behind the trees. Kyle stretched his legs out in front of him and rested both arms over the back of the bench. He didn't try the sly put-your-arm-around-me move; he crooked his arm at the elbow and let it hang casually between us. We sat quietly, and for a moment I felt like an old couple, like those ones you see in rocking chairs on the front porch, sitting for hours and not talking but totally content. It was odd. But nice.

"So," he finally said. "I was wondering . . ."

Until then I'd been pretty relaxed considering I was out with a guy alone at sunset. But suddenly my pulse picked up. I didn't look at him or say anything.

"That dance is on Friday, right?" he asked.

"Yeah, I think it's this Friday," I said as if I didn't know.

"I bet Kristen has already got Tobias roped into going, huh?"

"You know my friends so well," I said. "She hasn't nailed him down yet, but believe me, she's working on it. She said if he doesn't ask her by Wednesday it's over between them. Of course, Tobias doesn't know this, but she thinks he should figure it out . . ."

I stopped, realizing I'd probably said too much. I didn't want Kyle to think I was like Kristen, that he had to ask me to the dance or we'd break up. Well . . . if we were even an official couple, that is.

"Wow, that's kind of harsh," Kyle said.

Yep. I'd said too much.

"She's mostly, like, joking around about it," I tried. Ugh. Talking to other people got me in way too much trouble. I couldn't have him thinking I agreed with Kristen's plan or that Kristen was a bad person for forcing—er, *encouraging* Tobias to make his own decision to dance or not to dance.

"What about you?" he said. "Do you want to go to the dance?"

"Me? I don't know." See? Me and words were not doing well, because of course I wanted to go to the dance. With him. But I didn't want him to think I was counting the days. I wasn't (much). I started messing with my hair, braiding the ends because *he was asking about the dance*! "It's kind of . . . you know . . . like some societal ritualistic thing . . ." What was I saying? That I did or didn't want to go?

"I mean with me," Kyle said. My heart stopped. I let go of my hair. "Do you want to go to the dance this Friday with me?"

His brown eyes stared directly into mine, the setting sun glowing on half his face. When I didn't answer, he looked away, back to where the trail began in the trees. "I wasn't sure if you were into that kind of thing. If you think it's dumb or lame—"

"No!" I said. "No, I don't think it's lame. And yes, I do want to go. With you, I mean." I knew I was blushing and I was totally smiling a big, stupid grin, but it was okay because now he was, too.

"Cool." He lowered his arms from the back of the bench. He angled his body slightly toward me and looked at me, my hair, my shoulder. He reached for my hand and leaned in, and in those two seconds I thought of something I hadn't thought of in all the is-he-my-boyfriend/are-we-going-to-the-dance drama: kissing. I'd never kissed a boy before. I didn't know how. I leaned away slowly, thinking how I wasn't ready, that I needed to prepare. I needed to talk to someone about this and . . . all of a sudden—butt, meet ground.

Yeah. I fell right off the bench and onto the grass.

"Are you okay?" Kyle asked, quickly standing and coming to help me up.

"Fine! Totally fine!" I said, politely ignoring his outstretched hand. I stood and dusted the dirt and grass off my butt, which did not hurt in the slightest, nuh-uh, no way. "The sun was . . . and it was shining . . . got in my eyes so I . . ." I was drowning. Totally drowning. I ended with the eloquent, "Yeah."

"It's just, you had a, uh . . ." Kyle motioned to his shoulder, then pointed to mine. "A ladybug. Looks like it's gone now." I brushed my shoulder, just in case. "You want to head back?"

"Yeah, sure."

Had I just blown a moment? I wondered if I should reach out and hold his hand and show him how calm and sophisticated I was. We were going to the dance together, after all. I guess we really were a couple now? Just the thought made me start to blush, so scratch that for now. Instead I said the first thing that popped into my mind. "Is Jonah taking Eve to the dance?"

"I'm not sure." He tucked his hands back in his pocket as we took a different route back to my house. I can happily report that it's the long way back, which meant he didn't think I was crazy with my bench-flying routine. "Eve's got that friend in town so he doesn't really know."

"No, yeah, of course," I said as if the answer didn't matter.

"Have you guys talked at all?" he asked.

I shook my head. "Well, yes, we've *talked*. But nothing real. I saw her after school today with that friend. I don't know . . . it gave me a bad feeling. Like her friend didn't like me and maybe was convincing Eve to ditch me completely."

Just saying it made me feel terrible all over again. *Maybe Marla wasn't being mean,* I thought. *Maybe she was complimenting my blouse, or . . .*

"Don't worry," he said. "I'm sure it's all going to work out."

We exited the park onto a small street with a couple of tiny shops and secluded restaurants. As we passed one of the restaurants, a fancy seafood placed called The Kitchen, I almost slammed into a woman.

"Oh my gosh," I said, stopping short before it was a full-on collision.

"Mickey," a familiar voice said. When I caught my breath, I realized it was Giancarlo. I took another look at the woman and when she smiled, it hit me. It was Ana—the woman from the salon yesterday. What was she doing out with Giancarlo?

"Hey!" I said. "What's up?"

"Just having a little dinner." His eyes darted to Kyle, and panic set in. Giancarlo was not a subtle person. At all. Like, ever a day in his life. Especially when I was caught walking around town at almost-dark with a boy I'd been talking to him about.

Ana eyed me and said, "Your hair is looking exceptionally shiny and healthy." A knowing grin grew on her lips.

"Really?" I asked, touching my long hair. "You can tell?"

"It does look good, Mickey," Giancarlo agreed. "Did you use that new shine serum we have at the salon?"

That morning I had tried the cold water trick Ana had recommended for shiny and frizz-free hair. My head almost froze off doing it, but I guess it'd worked.

"No," I said to Giancarlo. "I tried something else."

"You sure did," Ana said with a wink.

This lady knew a thing or two about hair. Which of course meant that I suddenly liked her very much.

"I'm Ana," she said to Kyle.

"Oh, sorry!" I said. "This is my—this is Kyle," I stumbled.

"Hey," he said, raising his hand in a quick wave.

I swore Giancarlo raised a brow at Kyle, so I quickly said to Ana, "I guess you got your appointment with Giancarlo?"

"Yes, I'm all set," Ana said. "Finally, I meet the great Giancarlo and I get to dine with him! I don't want to be dramatic, but this is a pretty big deal for me."

Giancarlo practically levitated in his black-and-white wingtips.

"Oh, Ana, you're too much. Go on, tell me more," he joked, and they both broke into giddy laughs. "Wait, can you see it?" He stretched his hands out from his head. "It's growing. You're giving me a big head!"

I couldn't help but laugh, too. Even Kyle did. Giancarlo loved being the center of attention. I know most people enjoy praise, but to Giancarlo it was like a curling iron to straight hair—instant pop.

"Giancarlo," I said. "Make sure you give Ana the works." I felt a little show-offy with Kyle standing there. He was totally getting to see me in action, talking style with stylists. I'm sure I looked very mature. "Give her one of your famous scalp massages, which I've only heard are fantastic. Not like I'd actually know or anything, since you've never given me one."

"That's a great idea, honey," Giancarlo said. "Mickey, you haven't been practicing those massages on this boy's head, have you?"

"Um, we gotta go," I said, stepping away while tugging on Kyle's arm. I should have known Giancarlo would get me before I ever got him.

"No salon work outside the salon!" he called as I turned away, and there was a glint in his eyes that said he was really enjoying seeing me frazzled. With Giancarlo I sometimes understood what it was like to have a brother.

"It was nice seeing you again, Ana," I called. "See you at the salon!"

They waved good-bye as Kyle and I practically ran

around the corner in the direction of home. Sometimes Giancarlo was worse than my dad. I decided right then and there that I'd keep all boys hidden from GC and Dad forever. Or at least as long as I could.

CHAPTER 8

"So, about the dance."

"What dance?"

Which is pretty much what I should have expected Jonah to say. But because he's my best friend, I let it go.

"*The* dance, this Friday," I clarified as we walked to school the next morning.

"Oh, right. What about it?"

"Guess who asked me to go with him last night?"

"If you're lucky, Adam Kennemore," he said.

For the record, Adam Kennemore is in our grade and he is gross. He's not a nose picker—he's an *ear* picker. You decide which is worse.

Instead of indulging Jonah with any kind of response, I said, "Kyle asked me. And I said yes. How about that?"

"That's cool. He told me last night he was going over to ask you," Jonah said. "Did he have to meet your parents?"

"Just Dad, and we left right after," I said. "We walked to the park and hung out for a little while." I thought of the ladybug incident. I still wasn't sure if that was a true story or a cover-up for what expectations Kyle might have. Did he expect me to fork over a kiss now that we were sort of, kind of, pretty much, definitely together? I realized that here in Jonah I had a real, live boy to ask such things—if I had the guts. I figured, like usual, I'd start by easing him in. "I totally embarrassed myself when I thought he was leaning in for a kiss but really he was just trying to flick a bug off me. I kind of freaked out."

"Why?"

"Because," I said. "I've never kissed a guy." I know Jonah is my best friend and all, but he's still a guy, and this was already an embarrassing conversation.

"I'm sure it'll be fine," he said, almost dismissively.

"Yeah, I know. I just . . . I don't know. About kissing. You know?"

He looked at me sideways. "If you're asking me to show you how to kiss, you can seriously forget it," he said, inching away from me the slightest bit.

"Jonah, please!" I said, gagging on the inside. "That is *not* what I'm asking."

"Then what *are* you asking? There's nothing to it. You just put your lips together and . . . I don't know, *kiss*."

My face heated up. This was not at all how I wanted to talk about this. Best friend or not, I needed to talk to a girl about this—that much was crystal clear. I had a ton of questions. Do we just mush our mouths together? Wiggle our lips? Open our mouths . . . ?

Ack! I couldn't bear it. "It's fine, forget it," I said. "What about Eve? I mean, are you guys going to the dance together?"

"Not if I can help it." He bent to pick up a stick on the sidewalk, then tossed it into the street.

I really missed Eve.

"So you're not going? What about Eve?"

"She's got her friend in town. So that means I've—" He crouched and leaned quickly to his right, quickly to his left, and back again.

"What are you doing?"

"Dodging bullets!"

We started walking again. "Jonah, can you be serious?"

"About a school dance? No."

"Then how about be serious about me and Eve?" I asked.

He bent to pick up another stick, but this time he didn't throw it. "Okay," he said. "Talk."

I loved how Jonah could flip from his obnoxious boy self to his good friend self so easily.

"It's just that . . . well, first of all, that was weird of

you guys yesterday at lunch."

He broke the stick in half. "I know."

"We all knew you weren't studying or whatever you told us. It's because Eve doesn't want to be around me, isn't it?"

"I'm sorry, Mickey," he said, tossing half the stick into a yard we passed. I'm sure their lawn mower would be thrilled to find it. "I didn't mean to lie to you. It's just that . . . well, you're pretty much right. She's still mad."

"Did she tell you I met her friend yesterday? Marla?"

"She mentioned it," he said. Then nothing.

"Did she say anything else?" I had to know everything she said about me and *how* she said it.

"She didn't, I promise. She just mentioned it, like, in passing," he said. "And if it makes you feel any better, we're not for sure *not* going to the dance. She has to see about Marla first. But you really should talk to her. Make the first move. I'm sure she'll come around."

"I've already tried," I said. "Now she's so busy with her friend."

We approached the school, and finally I admitted, "I just feel weird around her. Them. Marla *and* Eve."

"Just remember," Jonah said. "Eve is still your friend."

84

But as we walked into the school, I wondered if that was still true.

I decided I needed a new plan. I'd up my efforts to be nice and normal with Eve. She had to feel comfortable around me again, and there was no better way to do that than by having some easy, casual conversation with her.

But when I walked into the cafeteria, I stopped dead in my tracks. What was Marla doing there? In our school? Sitting next to Eve for lunch?

I slowly walked to our table, noticing with an intense pang of jealousy that Marla was sitting in my seat. In the seconds-long encounters I'd had with Marla, I knew she was wary of me. I knew Eve had told her what I'd done.

I slipped into a seat next to Jonah and across from Eve and Marla. "Hey, guys," I said, forcing a smile as if I weren't being kicked in the gut. "Hey, Marla. What are you doing here?"

"Hey," she said, a steady look in her eyes. "Just having some lunch."

"Cool," I said, looking between her and Eve. I didn't know random people could just show up at school for lunch.

"The school doesn't care as long as you ask," Eve

said as if knowing what I'd been thinking.

We sat silently for a moment as I took out my lunch. I had the feeling that if I weren't there, they'd be talking. Not necessarily about me, but it seemed clear that my presence made things awkward. Where were Kristen and Lizbeth when I needed them? They were probably off cornering the boys in some dark hallway, forcing them into committing to the dance.

After taking a long gulp of water, I asked Eve, "You excited about the dance on Friday? Marla, will you still be in town?"

Eve shook her head. "She'll be in town but I don't know if she's coming."

Kyle came over to our table just then, noted our seating arrangement and new guest, then sat beside me. I smiled and said, "Hey." In the midst of the stilted conversation, it was even better to see him than usual.

Kyle smiled back. "Hello," he said in a quiet voice, meant just for me to hear. Blood rushed to my head and my heart raced. He leaned around me and said, "Hey, guys."

Bags thumped onto the table, and Kristen and Lizbeth both sat down with a heavy *thud*. I guess my moment for a friendly chat with Eve had passed.

"We're finished," Kristen said, disgusted. She did a double take seeing Marla sitting at our table. "Hey," she said.

"Guys, this is my friend Marla," Eve announced. "She's in town from Ridgeley seeing family and also hanging out with me. It's her spring break," she clarified.

Everyone said hello, and I could just feel Kristen's and Lizbeth's eyes shooting toward me for my reaction.

"So," I said to Kristen. I needed the attention to be off me. "What are you finished with?"

"Tobias," Kristen said, practically spitting his name. "We broke up. He acted like such a jerk when I told him he needed to ask me to the dance. He got all, 'Why are you telling me what to do?' And I was all, 'I'm not telling you what to do, I'm telling you what you should have already done.' He refused to ask me but get this—he said it didn't mean that we weren't together. I was just like, 'You know what? I don't need this in my life. We are so over.'" She pushed her lunch away and leaned her elbows on the table. "So that's that."

Normally, I would chuckle a little at Kristen's antics, maybe reach out and touch her wrist while plastering on a concerned face, all because I knew this would blow over by the end of the day. The difference today was Marla. Judging by the way she reacted to meeting me yesterday, I had a feeling she thought I was a terrible friend. I had to show her otherwise.

"You must be in so much pain," I said to Kristen.

Worrying I sounded like a soap opera actor, I said, "I mean, are you *okay*?" I gave her an extra look of concern.

"I will be as soon as he gets a clue," she said.

"I'm here for you if you want to talk about it," I said.

Kristen looked at me and said, "That's what I'm doing, Mickey. Talking about it. Which, by the way, won't make Tobias use his brain. When will he figure out that if he just does what I tell him, everything will be fine?"

"What about you?" I asked Lizbeth. "Are you out, too?"

"Matthew hasn't asked me yet," Lizbeth said, sealing and unsealing her bag of strawberries. I knew she wanted him to ask her and was probably getting worried that he hadn't yet.

"I'm sure he will," I said. "Some guys just take a little longer."

"She won't demand an answer from him like I did," Kristen said. "But listen: Just because Tobias and I are through doesn't mean I'm not going to the dance. Please. I am so going and looking hotter than ever. He'll be sorry he didn't ask me."

To Eve I said, "Now you have to come to the dance! We can't leave Kristen alone." I thought of last night with Kyle, and the fool I made of myself when he tried to kiss me—or brush the bug off my shoulder. The dance seemed like just the place he'd actually try to kiss me and if I still wasn't ready by then, I'd need my friends to help keep us from being alone. "Maybe we should all go together. It'll be much more fun that way. And Marla, you can come, too!"

"To the dance?" she said skeptically. "I don't think I want—"

"I'm not even sure if the school will let her," Eve broke in. I had the sinking feeling that even when Marla didn't finish a sentence she was on the verge of insulting me. I guess it was a good thing that Eve interrupted—she still liked me enough for that. "Since she's not a student here. Anyway, I just want to get this science project done. Then I'll think about the dance."

Jonah said, "Hey, whatever you want to do is cool with me. Dance, no dance, as a group, alone. Whatever. Tell me what you want and I'll do it."

"Eve, you're so lucky," Kristen said. "Why can't Tobias be more like Jonah?"

Eve smiled, her cheeks and across her forehead blushing bright-pink. "He's okay, I guess," she said, giving him a smile. "Hey, does anyone else have Ms. Howard for science?" We all shook our heads no. "We have to come up with an invention by Friday. I have no idea what I'm going to do."

"I told her I'd help her with it," Marla said. "She keeps saying she'll get it done. We don't have to go out every night, Eve."

"But I want to hang out with you," Eve said.

"I can help you," I said. "We can work on it at lunch. Go to the library and brainstorm or something."

"We could just as easily work in the evenings," Marla said. "If Eve weren't such a good host, that is." The girls smiled at each other. It looked like at any second they'd hug it out and have a moment right there at the table. Ugh.

"I'll try to think of things for you," I said.

"That'd be cheating," Marla said.

"No, it wouldn't," I said, bristling at the accusation. "It's just that it's clear she's distracted in the evenings."

"Eve, you're smart," Lizbeth broke in. I realized everyone was looking between me and Marla. "You'll come up with something."

"Yeah," Kristen said, taking Lizbeth's cue, trying to calm the conversation. "By Friday at the dance it'll all be done and we can just relax and party."

Kyle shifted in his seat, and his thigh brushed up against mine. He left it there, our thighs touching, and my face heated up.

"I have an idea!" I said, casually shifting my leg away. "We should all get dressed together at the salon. I bet my mom would let us use the products.

Oh! That reminds me, Eve, Giancarlo said he'd do your hair. Mom is giving me a blowout—it's going to be all long and straight, and Giancarlo said he'd make yours curly. How cute would that be?"

"What about Marla?" she said.

Oops. I honestly hadn't meant to not invite her, right to her face. "You're invited, too, of course," I improvised. "I'm sure we can get you an appointment if you want one."

"Um, maybe," she said, clearly unsure. "But I really don't want to bother Eve with this too much right now. She's really stressed about her science project, so maybe we can just get back to you on the whole dance thing?"

"Yeah, she's right," Eve said. "Is that okay?"

"Of course," I said. "Absolutely. Whatever you need."

As lunch ended, I got the distinct feeling that Marla and I were playing a high-stakes game at who was a better friend to Eve. And she had just won this round.

CHAPTER 9

Eve and Marla left the cafeteria with Jonah, and I walked out with Kyle. He didn't say much. We just walked to my English classroom, and he said he'd find me after school.

Eve was already at her desk when I got to class. She smiled at me as I walked to my seat, and I tried not to smile back too eagerly. I needed to calm down. No one liked a desperate friend.

She leaned over and asked, "So how's it going with Kyle?"

"Great!" I cheered. "It's going good."

She nodded and got out her notebook and pen as the class settled in. I wanted to ask her if she and Jonah had kissed yet. Probably. Maybe I could ask her advice on the whole thing as a way to get things back to normal *and* to gather the info I needed. *I should just do it*, I told myself. *Just ask her.*

"Hey," I said, leaning toward her a bit. In the moment it took Eve to turn to face me, I got a flash of an image of her and Jonah kissing and *oh my gosh* that is just *not* something I wanted to see, even in my head. And then suddenly, the image was burned there. I couldn't get it out.

"Yeah?" Eve said, waiting.

"I just, um . . . do you want to do something together after school? Marla, too, of course."

It was a decent save, but then I realized Eve had just been worrying about getting her project done.

"That'd be awesome," she said, "but I'm meeting her at the Berkshire Museum, plus I really have to work on my project."

"No! Right, of course!" I said. Eve probably thought I was a terrible listener, which would also mean I was a horrible friend. I may have been trying, but clearly I wasn't trying hard enough. Or maybe I was trying too hard? Was that possible?

"Lizbeth! Hey—wait up!"

The moment I saw Lizbeth down the hall, I knew she was the one I had to talk to.

"I have something serious I need to talk to you about," I said to her. "Can you go to the diner after school? Cheese fries and milkshakes on me."

"Ooh, my favorite foods plus total intrigue? How could I say no?" she said. "But can it be a half hour after school? I have to meet with my history teacher about a project we have coming up. Want to wait for me here or meet me there?"

"I'll meet you there," I said. "And thanks."

"Anytime," she said.

After school, before I could even get out the front door, Eve caught up to me.

"I'm glad I caught you," she said.

"Hey," I said. Seeing her flushed face, I continued, "Everything okay?"

"Yeah, it's great," she said. "It's just, um . . . are you going home?"

"Not quite yet," I said as we walked out the doors.

"I was wondering if maybe you wanted to go with me to meet Marla," she said, and I was struck by how nervous she seemed. She looked like I'd felt earlier in English class. "The museum is supposed to be pretty good. I thought it might be fun."

I slowed my walk. Was she asking me to go with them now? Why hadn't she in class? Had she talked to Marla and gotten it cleared with her first? I didn't like the idea of that—not at all.

"Um, well . . . ," I began, my brain scrambling. I couldn't ditch one friend for another.

"I mean, if you can't it's no big deal," Eve said,

her face burning pink. I couldn't believe it—she really was nervous.

"No, I'd like to, it's just, I already have plans," I said. "Lizbeth and I are going to the diner to hang out. You guys could stop by later? Maybe we'll still be there." Totally unlikely, but if she was inviting me to hang out I wanted to say yes.

"It's okay," she said. "We'll do something some other time."

"Thanks for asking me," I said. "Really."

"Yeah, sure," Eve said, looking off toward the road like she really wanted to bolt.

"Hey! Mickey!" We turned to see Kyle running toward us. "I thought I'd missed you."

"Hey, Kyle," I said. If there was such a thing as grinning on the inside, I was totally doing that.

"Oh, I'm sorry," he said, glancing to Eve. "I didn't mean to interrupt. I was just going to see if I could walk home with you. I'm heading in that direction, anyway—to Jonah's."

"Yeah, sure," I said. Then noticed Eve's face—her mouth dropped open. She looked at me like I had just told her a big, fat lie about the diner. "No! Sorry, I mean I'm not going home," I said to Kyle. "I'm going to Camden Way. To meet Lizbeth. Want to walk me there?"

"Sure," Kyle said. "Wherever you're going."

"I gotta go," Eve said.

Oh my gosh. Eve totally thought I was a huge liar, I just knew it.

"No, wait," I said, although I wasn't sure what I wanted her to wait for. "Let's make plans to do something later this week."

"I have that science project," she said.

"Okay," I said. "Well, maybe if you need help or anything just let me know."

She looked between me and Kyle. Finally, she nodded and said, "See you guys tomorrow."

I watched Eve go, feeling like I had just made things worse between us.

"You okay?" Kyle asked.

"Yeah. I don't know," I said as we started our walk to Camden Way. "It was weird. In English I asked if she wanted to hang out, but she said she couldn't. But then, just now, she invited me to hang out with her and Marla, but I've already made plans. I think she's upset—maybe she thinks I'm jerking her around?"

"I'm sure she doesn't think that," Kyle said. "And if you're talking, that's good, right?"

"That's true," I said. "But then when you asked to walk home with me and I said yes, I think she thought I was lying about not being able to hang out with her."

"I think you're reading way too much into it," Kyle said. "She just needed a little time, that's all."

"Maybe," I said. "With Marla in town it's just such bad timing. Eve once told me that they'd drifted apart when she moved here. I wonder what made Marla decide to spend her spring break here. Do you think that's strange?"

He shrugged. "I don't know. Not really. Maybe like you, Marla missed hanging out with her. Eve's a good friend to have—she seems like she'd be missable."

"Yeah. Eve is totally *missable*." I smiled.

Kyle just *got* it. I didn't have to do a lot of explaining of things to him. Plus, he listened and seemed to really, truly care. I mean, come on—what else was I supposed to want in a guy?

At the crosswalk we watched the traffic slowly roll by and when the walk sign flashed on, Kyle took my hand in his and guided me across the street. I wondered if he'd let go once we were safely on the sidewalk, but he didn't and I was glad. His hand wasn't all sweaty or rough like I thought a boy's might be, either. I'm not saying he wore lotion mittens at night, but they felt great. I gently squeezed his hand, like a little message saying I liked this. He gave me a squeeze back.

During the last few blocks to the diner, Kyle told me a story about seeing our principal at the bowling alley with his family and how weird it was to see him out of his suit and in those shoes. I told him about the time Ms. Carter came into Hello, Gorgeous! and I spilled a soda all over her well-toned arms and legs.

We were almost to the diner when Kyle said, "Wait, come here." He pulled me into a narrow walkway that led to an alley for the shops on Camden Way. Weeds grew between the cobblestones beneath our sneakers, and he gently led me back against the redbrick wall. The noises of the main street were slightly muffled, and his voice was that much quieter when he said, "Is this okay?"

I felt my head nodding yes but I had no idea what was going on.

He took both my hands in his and held them down by our thighs. He ran a thumb across my knuckle in a way that was probably meant to be soothing but my heart was pounding so hard and my mind raced. Now I knew the reality of the moment that was upon me: the kiss.

I wasn't ready. I was moments away from talking to Lizbeth about this. It couldn't happen *now*—it just couldn't. I'd mess it up, do the wrong thing, and scare him off forever. I'd be known as Mickey the Terrible Kisser and that would follow me through high school and college. No one would ever ask me out again and I'd die alone with cats climbing all over my face.

He looked at my lips, slightly parting his own. I wanted to pull back just the slightest bit but my back was against the wall—there was nowhere to go. Kyle leaned his head slightly to the left and then . . .

"I just wanted you to know that I really like hanging out with you," he said. "I'm really glad I'm your boyfriend."

Okay, wait. How did I go from terrified to sa-*woon* in under five seconds? I wanted to melt. I wanted to kiss him.

Almost. I wanted to talk to someone about it first.

"I'm really glad I'm your girlfriend," I said, my voice quivering the slightest bit.

He smiled this small, crooked smile that showed a dimple I'd never seen before. "Ready to go?"

No, I thought.

"Yeah," I said.

Still holding hands, we walked back to the sidewalk and up the few steps to the diner. He opened the door for me. I saw Lizbeth sitting at a booth and she waved me over.

"Thanks for the walk," I said to Kyle. He wouldn't try to do it right here in front of the old hostess, would he?

"See you tomorrow," he said, giving my hand a final squeeze before letting go and heading out the door.

When I got to Lizbeth's booth I collapsed into it.

"What was all that about?" she asked with a wide grin on her face like she totally knew.

"That," I said, "was about a boy."

"Then we better get extra cheese on those fries."

CHAPTER 10

"You have to tell me everything you know about kissing," I said to Lizbeth after I filled her in on my walks with Kyle—today's and yesterday's—and my complete panic at the thought of a kiss. "I'm not uncomfortable if you're not."

"I'm not uncomfortable," she said, biting into an extracheesy, extracrispy fry.

"I thought about talking to Kristen about it but I know she's got enough boy problems right now as it is," I said, pulling the black-and-white shake closer to me and taking a long sip. "Plus, I was afraid of what she'd tell me. Probably something involving swirls and rotations."

"She once told Tobias that she would allow him to kiss her cheek. He was like, 'What is this? The 1800s?'" She laughed. "He passed on her offer."

"So," I began, telling myself to not be nervous or

feel stupid. There were no stupid questions, right? Lowering my voice so the old ladies in the booth behind us couldn't hear, I said, "Can you, like, describe how to kiss someone?" I honestly wanted to hide my face in my hands, but I had to be brave. It was probably just as embarrassing for Lizbeth. But better to be embarrassed with a friend than with my boyfriend.

"Well," she said. "You basically just touch your lips together with, like, a little pressure. And I guess you move them around some, like sort of opening and closing your mouth. When you want to go a little advanced you can—"

"Okay!" I said. "Got it!" I couldn't think about advanced anything. I just couldn't do it. No way.

"It's not that bad," Lizbeth said. "Sometimes it's awkward at first—"

"More awkward than this conversation?" I joked.

She smiled. "Maybe. But there's nothing to be afraid of. It's easy. And nice."

I wiped my hands on my napkin. "Okay, but here's what I was thinking. And promise not to laugh."

"Swear."

"I was thinking—if I'm still not ready to do the kissing thing when the dance comes around—that I would wear really thick, shiny, goopy lip gloss. What do you think?"

Lizbeth stopped midreach for another fry. "Mickey, I don't know a lot about boys. Honestly, I don't. But I do know one thing."

"What is it?"

She leaned forward and said, "If a boy wants to kiss you, he'll kiss you. Even if you have mud on your lips."

"But I'm talking about that kind that comes in the squeezy tube. The *really* sticky kind."

She shook her head. "It won't work. Listen," she said. "If you're not ready, you don't have to kiss him. All you have to do is say, 'Kyle, I'm not ready.' He is one of the best guys we know—he'll be cool about it." She eyed me for a moment. "What's really bothering you?"

I sighed. "I don't know. He's my first boyfriend. I'm afraid of making a fool of myself."

"You are not going to make a fool of yourself," she said.

"Maybe. But it just seems like a couple months ago I was whopping Kyle's butt in video games and now I'm thinking about kissing him. I haven't exactly been planning for this."

"The first time I kissed a boy," Lizbeth said, "I totally felt the same way. I was so nervous, my heart was about to jump out of my chest. But it's like, once you get over that anticipation part, it's not a big deal. I promise."

"Hopefully. I don't plan on avoiding him forever."

"In that case," she said, "here's my advice."

Now I was the one leaning forward, listening closely through the clattering of plates in the background.

"Just go with it," she said.

I waited for more. When I realized she wasn't saying anything else, I said, "That's it? Just go with it?"

"Kissing is a no-brainer, but you only realize it once you've done it."

"So what am I supposed to do until then?" I asked.

She shrugged. "Eat lots of breath mints."

We laughed and settled back into the grub.

"So, while we're on the subject," I said. "Have you and Matthew . . . ?"

She kept her face turned down toward the table, but it didn't hide her smile. "Have we what?"

"Oh, please! Have you guys made out, kissed, macked down?"

She laughed. "'Macked down'? Did you just make that up?"

"Maybe," I said. "And I'm going to take this reaction as a yes."

"Fine," she said. "Yes, we have kissed. Just twice, though."

"Ooh la la," I teased.

She stirred her milkshake and said, "I really like him. He's supersmart and totally hot and is probably the only guy in school who can handle Tobias's ego. That means he's patient, too."

"You're saying he's more than just a good argyle sweater?" I teased.

She grinned. "Much more. I'm not freaking out over him asking me to the dance because I know he will."

"So you're definitely not going with Kristen's tactics?"

"No way," she said. "I love her, but she operates on an entirely different level."

"I'm afraid of her level," I said. "I'm not sure I'd ever be ready for that kind of intensity. And fighting."

"You don't have to be," Lizbeth said. "I know I'll never be like that. Besides, I'd be shocked if Matthew didn't ask me—that's how sure I am that he will."

"I like your confidence," I said.

"It comes in handy now and then," she said. "How are things going with you and Eve?"

The corners of my mouth pulled down at the mention of her name. "They're okay, I guess. I was actually talking to Kyle about it on the way over here."

"What'd he say about it?"

"He thinks she'll come around. She just needs a little time."

"Smart guy," Lizbeth said.

"I've only been around her friend Marla a couple of times but I get the feeling she doesn't like me."

I expected her to say, "Please! I'm sure she's just shy," or something like that. But she didn't. And her silence told me she wanted to say something more but didn't know how.

"Hey," I asked. "Do you know something?"

"No," she said, shaking her head. "I don't know anything. Honestly. It's just that, well, the BFF thing is tricky, even if they're not official best friends anymore. It's a tough force to crack through, like a shared history or something."

"Great," I said. "So you're saying it's hopeless."

"No," Lizbeth said. "But I think the key to Eve is through Marla."

"I'm not kissing up to her, if that's what you mean."

"Please," she said. "I would never in a thousand recommend that. But if you can earn Marla's trust, then I bet Eve will start to see that she can trust you again, too."

I thought about that. I knew right away that Kyle was a good guy because he was Jonah's friend. I knew Jonah would never hang around anyone shady. Maybe the same was true with Eve and Marla.

"So I should join forces with Marla, huh?" I said. It might be a good idea, but I wasn't 100 percent thrilled with it.

"Just a suggestion," she said, popping a now-soggy fry in her mouth.

"Yeah, well I have a suggestion, too," I said. "You. Me. Kristen. Dress shopping. What do you say? Thursday after school? I have to work Wednesday."

"All I heard was *shopping* so yes, I'm in."

I was fighting to get back one of my best friends, but it was comforting knowing that I still had an army of great ones by my side, ready to be there for me when I needed them most.

Lizbeth and I walked out of the diner—she turned left and I went right.

I started my walk past the shops on Camden Way, thinking about everything Lizbeth had said. She was probably right about Marla, and I should try to get in with her. Not in a deceitful way because honestly, if Eve liked her and had been friends with her all those years, she had to be a good person, right? Based on my Kyle-as-Jonah's-friend theory, anyway.

Suddenly, I paused. Standing outside Suds en Provence, the fancy soap shop up ahead, was the girl of the moment herself. That's the thing about small towns—if there's someone you want to avoid seeing, even just for a breather, you'll probably be out of luck. It was like a statistical fact.

I sucked up all my pride and headed straight for her. I wanted to cross the street to avoid her but knew Lizbeth's idea was a good one.

Marla was crouched down on her heels below the front window listening to music on her phone. She wore a black leather headband, her short hair spiking out of the top of it. I had to admit, I'd never seen someone wear a headband so tough.

"Marla—hey," I said, once I was standing in front of her. She looked up at me, then slowly stood up and took out her earbuds.

"Hey," she said. "What's up?" She wrapped the cord around her phone like she was settling in for a long talk that I'm sure she wanted no part of. I kind of wanted to tell her not to do me any favors, but reminded myself that I was there for Eve, not Marla.

"What are you doing hanging out here?" I asked.

"Eve's inside," she said, motioning into the shop with a nod of her head. "She's getting some bath salts for her grandmother or something."

"They have some really great stuff here," I said, looking at the window display full of handmade soaps made with rose essences and kiwis and mangos. "I never knew soap could be so fancy."

"The smell was making me sick."

Some kids skated by behind me, and Marla watched them go as if she longed for them to take her away.

Or maybe I was projecting. "How was the museum?" I asked.

She lifted one shoulder in a shrug as if she couldn't be bothered to lift both. "Okay. I mean, it was a museum."

I put my hands in my pockets to avoid the desire to reach out and rattle her neck. The Berkshire Museum happened to be really interesting, thanks very much. Did she have to be so negative about everything?

"Are you and Eve at least having fun?" I pressed on.

"Yeah," she said. "It's good to see her. I hadn't realized how much I missed her."

"I'm glad you got to come then."

She didn't say anything, just eyed me for a moment. I shifted under her gaze. "You know," she began, "just because Eve and I haven't talked much lately doesn't mean we're not good friends. Because we are."

"I know," I said, even though I didn't. What was she getting at?

"She has had a hard time since moving here. Unnecessarily. *Because of you.*"

I could barely move. If a tornado swept down Camden Way I'd probably have stayed glued to the sidewalk. I was angry that she would talk about my business with Eve and embarrassed that I even had such business with Eve. I didn't respond, just kept my gaze even with hers.

"Look," she said, more gently this time. "I'm just looking out for her. Okay?"

A chiming bell shook me from my paralyzed state. We both turned to see Eve walking out of the shop. Only then did I start to breathe again.

"Mickey?" Eve questioned as she came up to us. "What are you doing here? I thought you had plans."

"I, uh," I began, realizing how dry my throat was. I cleared it and tried again. She probably thought she was yet again busting me in a lie. "I did. I just got done hanging out with Lizbeth. I'm on my way home now."

Eve looked between us and asked Marla, "You guys been out here long?"

"Nah," Marla said. "Just a couple of minutes."

"Cool." Eve nodded. "We're heading back to my house. I guess I'll see you tomorrow."

"Yeah," I said. Despite the tension, I was sad to see her go, to know she didn't want to spend any more time with me. "See you at school."

I walked home alone, wondering how long the damage would last between us. I understood Marla wanting to protect Eve—I wanted to protect her, too. But from what? Me? All I knew was that I missed her, and I needed a way to fix this.

CHAPTER 11

Instead of going home, I went straight to Jonah's. I wasn't feeling great about my run-in with Marla and needed to see my friend. I knew that even if he didn't have a solution, just being with Jonah would assure me that I wasn't the world's worst friend.

"What do you think about Marla?" I asked Jonah as we lounged on the couch in the game room and watched TV.

"I don't know," he said, staring at the screen as a girl sang a country song on the competition show we couldn't get enough of. "She's all right."

"You don't think she's kind of, I don't know, bullheaded?"

"You mean like a bully?" he asked.

"No," I said. "That's not what I said." The last thing I wanted was to be accused of calling her *that*.

"So what *are* you saying?" Jonah asked. "This

girl sounds like a dying whale," he said of the girl on the show.

"I'm just saying," I began, trying to find the right words, "that she seems a bit protective of Eve."

"Why wouldn't she be?" Jonah asked. "She's her friend."

"I mean protective against me," I clarified.

"Yeah, well. Then it makes even more sense."

"Jonah!" I said. I couldn't believe he'd just sided with her. "Could you be a little more harsh?"

He had the decency to finally pull his eyes away from the TV and look at me. "Sorry, Mick. But don't you think that Eve probably told Marla everything that's happened between you two?"

"I *know* she did," I said. "I ran into Marla tonight. Alone."

"What happened?"

"She confronted me about Eve. She said just because she wasn't around didn't mean that she and Eve aren't good friends, and that Eve has had an unnecessarily hard time since she moved here because of me. She said that."

"Well, it's probably true," he said.

"Thanks for the reassurance."

"Sorry, but seriously—if Marla had done what you did to Eve, how would you treat her right now?"

Instead of answering, I stared back at the TV. I wasn't ready to admit he was right.

"Marla is probably the perfect person for her to talk to," he continued. "Eve is still somewhat new here, and if one of her new friends did her wrong, she might feel safer talking to an old friend who is totally outside the situation."

How was it possible that he could know so much about girls? I couldn't believe it. But it depressed me knowing how right he was—and how lonely Eve must be feeling. I wanted to be there for her, but I was the one who caused the whole mess in the first place.

"She still hasn't said anything to you about me?" I asked.

"I really haven't seen much of her all week. She's been hanging out with Marla and working on that science project."

"Protective, good friend Marla," I said. I wasn't being snarky. I was starting to think. It was possible that Marla was Eve's good friend because she was there for her—even when she was in a different town. Maybe I could learn a lesson from her.

I shivered at the thought.

"Look," Jonah said as the voting lines opened up for the show. He grabbed his phone and started texting in. "Marla's only here a couple more days. Try to play nice with her a little longer. You might actually see that she's not that bad. Who knows," he said, hitting SEND on his phone. "You might even like her."

I walked home across our yards to find Mom sitting at the kitchen table looking through magazines.

"Hey," she said, looking up at me. "How are things at the Goldmans'?"

"Good," I said, sitting down across from her.

She studied a page and said, "What do you think of this?" She turned the magazine to face me. The image was of a woman with a sort of bowl cut, but longer, to her shoulders.

"Meh," I said. "Not so much."

"Yeah," she said, turning the magazine back. "Me neither. So—dance on Friday, right?" She looked up at me, her eyes grinning.

"Yep," I said. "Going with Kyle."

"Ah, Kyle," she said. "Jonah's friend, right?" I nodded.

"How are you doing your hair?" she asked, an important question for sure.

"Giancarlo suggested a blowout," I said. "But a proper one this time. Not just straightening with a flatiron like last time."

"That was not your best look," Mom said, a true statement if there ever was one. "Maybe something pulled back but loose? A few pieces hanging down the side?"

"Yeah," I said, liking the idea. "I'll keep looking at styles in my magazines."

"Such a good client. I taught you well." She reached across the table and patted my hand. "So. Kyle, huh? He's pretty handsome."

"Mom . . . ," I said, trying not to smile. I knew he was good-looking, but . . . "You think he is?"

"Sure," she said, resting her chin on her hand. "Great head of hair like your father."

I put my hands on my face, feeling them turn hot. I'd never talked about boys with my mom before. "I guess," I said, wondering what it would feel like to kiss him, then turning even redder than before. "I'm heading up to my room," I told Mom before she started telling me about the first boy she kissed. *Ack* overload.

CHAPTER 12

"Is he looking?" Kristen asked Lizbeth.

She sat at our lunch table with her body angled toward Tobias's table, but her face turned away. She looked outstanding today in a fitted white tee with a large, black sequined heart covering the front, and her hair was loose and wild with a few thin braids hidden beneath the curls.

"He's not looking at you," Lizbeth said. "But other people are because you're acting weird."

"I'm not acting weird," Kristen said. "I'm acting like a person who doesn't care but happens to look amazing."

"You do look really nice today," I said.

"And you smell," Kyle said, his nose wrinkled. I poked his arm with my elbow. "I mean, nice. You smell really nice."

She was wearing a lot of perfume.

Kristen glared at Kyle, and I thought she might lose it. Instead she flipped her hair over her shoulder and stood up. "I'm going to get some Jell-O. Anybody want anything?" We all said no, and she walked off—headed to the lunch line, but making a big loop toward Tobias's table, walking right past him, her head held high. He glanced at her, watched her for a moment, then went back to talking to Matthew.

"That is not a good sign," Jonah said as we all watched her continue to the lunch line. I noticed her fists were clenched by her side.

Lizbeth looked over to the boys' table and said to me, "So, about the dance . . ."

"Yeah?"

"Matthew asked me to go. Last night," she said, beaming.

"Lizbeth! That's awesome!"

"Yeah, way to go, Lizbeth," Eve said from the other side of Jonah.

"How did you get him to ask you?" I said with an eye on Kristen, who was paying for her Jell-O and glancing-but-not-really at Tobias.

"I didn't do anything," Lizbeth said. "I knew he'd ask when he was ready. Last night he just called me up and asked." She shrugged like this was the most normal thing in the world.

"A phone call and everything," I said. "Impressive."

"I'm really happy for you," Eve said.

"Yeah, me too," I added. "So this means we can still all go together, right?" I looked around the table at Kyle, Lizbeth, Jonah, and Eve. Eve kept her eyes down on her sack lunch. I had no idea if it was on purpose, or my own paranoia.

Kristen came back and sat down with a satisfied grin. "Did you see that? He was totally checking me out. I could feel it. Kristen: one. Tobias: loser."

Lizbeth shook her head at her friend while Kristen ignored her. I guess sometimes it was better to believe your own hype.

"We were just talking about the dance on Friday," I said. "About us all going together, like we talked about."

Kristen and Lizbeth exchanged looks.

"Well . . . ," Kristen began.

"What?" I asked.

"It's just that," Lizbeth said, "Matthew is taking me to dinner before the dance."

"And once Tobias asks me, like he should have all along, I'm telling him we're going with them."

"Uh, you are?" Lizbeth asked.

"What about the rest of us?" I asked. "Don't you think it'll be more fun to go as a group?"

"We'll all meet up here at school," Lizbeth said. She gave me a quick nod of reassurance, knowing that I was nervous about kissing Kyle.

"Why don't you guys all go together?" Kristen said, indicating Eve, Jonah, me, and Kyle.

No one said anything. I wasn't even sure Kyle wanted to go as a group, Eve hated me, and Jonah was oblivious.

"Maybe," I said, trying to think of something to say. "Just depends."

"On what?" Kristen asked.

"Marla," Jonah spoke up. "She's not sure if she's going."

"Why?" I asked. "Are you doing something with her family that night?"

I leaned forward around Jonah to look at Eve's face. She looked uncomfortable, not looking up at any of us. Jonah reached over and put his hand on her back.

"No, it's just that she doesn't know anyone here," she said. "I don't want her to feel out of place."

"Of course not," Lizbeth said. "She's your friend— you don't want her to be uncomfortable. She's more important than a dance."

"I know," Eve said. "I just don't want anyone relying on me to make some group thing for the dance. Everyone should do their own thing."

"Which means," Kyle said playfully to me, "you might just be stuck with me." The way he looked at me carefully made me think that he really wasn't being playful—he was being honest.

"I'm not stuck," I said, trying to match his tone. "I'm glad!" Because I was—I really was. I was just nervous. Stupid kissing.

"I just want to make sure you're not trying to ditch me," he said.

"As long as you can still make it to level four of Combat Zone, you're okay with me," I said.

"Oh, sure," he said. "Love me for my video game skills only."

Okay, I fully blushed at the word *love*, even though I knew he didn't really mean *love* love. Instead of responding I decided to drop the whole thing.

"Eve, you okay?" Lizbeth asked. Eve rested her head in her hand, elbow on the table. She hadn't been eating her lunch.

"Yeah, you seem a little out of it," Kristen said.

She looked up at the group—not at me. "There is something else."

Did Marla tell her she shouldn't be friends with me? I felt a mild panic thinking Eve was about to confront me in front of everyone.

"It's just that," Eve began, "it's that science project I told you all about. The invention one? It's killing me."

"What have you come up with so far?" Jonah asked, and I was a little surprised he didn't know already. I guess he really hadn't seen much of her this week.

"A couple of lame ones," she said. "I tried to do a thing on global warming but I got all confused with carbon dioxide stuff. And then I thought about doing an experiment on peer pressure and behavioral changes but realized that has nothing to do with science."

"It sounds really interesting, though," Lizbeth said.

"Yeah," I added. I guess I wanted Eve to know I was listening and interested, too. (Well, I was!)

"It was Marla's idea," she said. "She's trying really hard to help me, but she's just not very good with the *science* part of the science project."

"Is there anything we can do?" Lizbeth asked. "Help you brainstorm ideas or something?"

"Or maybe you can talk to Ms. Howard and let her know you have a guest in town," Kristen suggested. "Maybe she'll let you turn it in after Marla leaves."

"Doubtful," Eve said.

I didn't like knowing Marla was getting in the way of Eve's grades. I tried to think of some way I could help her short of doing her science project for her. Or politely suggesting Marla leave town early.

Oh, I'm kidding! Relax.

"I have this one idea but it's not very good," she said. "For a pencil with a sharpener attached. You know, like how you can add an extra eraser to the tops

124

of pencils? But this would be a removable sharpener."

"That's a great idea," Lizbeth said. "I have a million dull pencils."

"Yeah, sounds like you're onto something," Kristen said.

"Thanks, guys," Eve said. "I'm still not sure about it. I have to sketch something out to show how it'll work. It just doesn't feel very inspiring."

"If there's anything we can do," I said, "let us know."

She didn't look at me when she said, "Thanks."

During the rest of lunch, I thought about my idea of getting Marla out of Eve's hair so she could concentrate on her project. Marla wasn't the only one who was protective of Eve. I was, too, and I could show her just how protective I could be.

As we left lunch, I thought of how I could talk to Eve again in English—maybe I could come up with an idea for her project during class.

"Mind if I walk with you?" Kyle asked as we headed out of the caf.

"Yeah, sure," I said, happy to be with him a bit longer. I wondered if he was going to hold my hand.

"I'm just wondering," he began.

"See you later, Mickey!" Lizbeth and Kristen called as they headed away from us down the hall.

"Bye, guys!" I called back.

"Just wondering," Kyle started again, "why you're,

like, pushing this group thing for the dance."

"I, um, thought you wanted to go with everyone?"

"I want to go with you," he said. "The group thing was your idea. You still want to go with me, right?"

"Of course!" I said. "Yes, I do."

"Because if you don't want to, you don't have to."

"Kyle, I promise I want to go. With you," I said. I wanted to add, *Please, please don't be mad or think I don't like you!* Everything was so complicated right now, but the one thing I knew was that I liked Kyle—a lot.

He nodded, then reached out and took my hand. "So we're cool?"

Warmth rushed through my body as he laced his fingers through mine. "Yeah," I said. "We're cool."

CHAPTER 13

Thanks to all the anxiety I felt about Eve and the kiss and Kyle asking me if I really wanted to go with him solo to the dance, the salon was the big, bright spot in my life. I was so glad it was finally my day to shadow Giancarlo so I could fill him in on all the drama. Yes, I had the whole Kyle kiss thing on my mind, but my biggest concern at the moment was Eve.

When I walked into the salon, Giancarlo was posing for a picture with what looked like a client he had just styled.

"Now if you want my autograph that'll cost you," he told the woman after Megan took the picture with a camera phone. "Just teasing! Tell all your beautiful lady friends about me—if they haven't already heard, that is."

The woman—she looked to be in her fifties with short, golden-blond hair—giggled and said, "Now don't forget us little people on your rise to the top."

"Darling, I'd never," he said, waving his hand at her. "Wait, what's your name again?"

They both broke into laughter as she said good-bye and headed home.

"Wow," I said as I walked over. "What's that all about?"

Megan rolled her eyes and said, "Aftershocks of *Berkshires Beauty*."

"Don't roll your eyes," Giancarlo told her. "We're just having fun."

"Uh-huh," Megan said, but she smiled back at him.

Before I could really get started working, Giancarlo called me over to his station.

"Come here, girl," he said. I walked over and he said, "You're mine today."

"To be your assistant?" I asked.

"Yep—if you're up for it," he said.

"Yes, of course!" I said. "Mom told me the other night."

"Have a seat, then," he said, gesturing to the stool he had set up next to his station. "You can hand me the foils."

Once I was settled, he didn't waste any time diving right into the important stuff.

"How are things with Kyle?" he asked.

"Good," I said, smiling. "He asked me to the dance."

"Good for you!" Giancarlo said. "Good for him. So I guess he's your boyfriend then, huh?"

I nodded. He was, and I was happy. I thought of what he said to me in the hall after lunch and how nervous I was about being alone with him.

"What's that look for?" he asked.

I looked at the woman in his chair, her face buried under a shiny dome of foil.

"She's not listening," Giancarlo said. "Are you, Francine?"

"Can't hear a thing," she replied.

Giancarlo said, "See?"

I knew the way things went in hair salons—you were practically expected to lay your problems out on your stylist—or in my case, the stylist I was shadowing.

Still, I lowered my voice so the whole salon wouldn't hear me. "I really like Kyle," I said. "But I'm just a little nervous about the *kissing* thing." Believe me, Giancarlo was the only adult in the universe I'd dare mention this to, but maybe he had some advice on how to avoid humiliating myself.

"Sweetheart, you listen to me," he began, and I leaned in closely. "Do not let that boy do anything until you're ready. Some boys have this expectation that just because they take a girl to the movies or a dance or whatever that they're *owed* something in return. Do not believe that. You don't have to do one single thing except say thank you and good night. You hear me?"

"Giancarlo," I said, more embarrassed than ever. "That's not what I'm talking about." I knew I didn't *have* to kiss him if I didn't want to—but I *wanted* to. The problem was knowing when and how.

"Just tell me you hear me," he said.

"Fine," I said. "I hear you." And I would never be asking Giancarlo for kissing advice again!

"Now," he said, satisfied. "Got a dress picked out yet?"

"No," I said. "My friends and I are going to the mall after school tomorrow."

"For a dance on Friday?" he asked. "That doesn't give you a lot of time."

"I know," I said. "But we've all been so busy."

"Just make sure whatever you choose looks good with a blowout. You did ask your mom for one, didn't you?"

I slapped my forehead with the heel of my hand. "Shoot! I totally forgot to ask Megan to put it in the books!" If it wasn't in the reservations system, it was likely not to happen.

Giancarlo smiled while picking up another foil from the tray beside his client. "No worries. Yesterday I went ahead and booked an appointment for Eve and you. So you're all set."

"Giancarlo, you are the best," I said, feeling appreciative of how nice he was and guilty at the same time. I still didn't know if Eve was even going to the dance, let alone whether she would accept an appointment from me. And I still had no idea what to do about Marla.

"What's that look for?" he asked.

"It's just . . . Eve," I said. "I'm not sure if she'll be coming in. You might want to take her off your schedule so you can book someone else."

"Mickey," he said, pausing from his color job to fix me with a stern look. Even though he wore a black shirt with white starbursts and pink, checkered pants, the look he gave me was of utmost authority.

"Yes?" I asked innocently.

"Don't make me pry it out of you," Giancarlo said, starting back up with the brush. "Spill."

"Well, Eve and I are kind of on the outs," I said.

"Something happen?" he asked.

"Something called I dyed her hair blue and then accidentally almost broke her and Jonah up." I knew Giancarlo wouldn't think anything bad of me, but his client, Francine, probably thought I was a terrible person.

"You're not talking?" he asked.

"We are a little bit," I said. "But her old best

131

friend, Marla, is in town."

"Her friend," he said, nodding, understanding completely.

"She's like Eve's bodyguard or something. She acts like because I hurt Eve once I'll do it again. But I won't. All I want is to be friends with Eve and show her that she can trust me. But now it's like Marla won't let me get anywhere near her."

"I'm sure she's just looking out for her friend the same way you would if the situation were reversed," he said. "There," he said to Francine, finishing up the last foil. "You're all set. To the dryers you go."

"Thanks for the talk, Giancarlo," I said.

"My station is always open to you," he said.

While Francine waited for her color to set, I carried on with my sweeping duties and helped out the other stylists. A bit later, after Giancarlo had rinsed Francine's hair and began to style it, Ana came in, waving at Giancarlo across the salon.

"Mickey, honey," Giancarlo said with a sigh when he saw her. "Could you go take care of her?"

"Yeah, sure," I said. "You okay?" He looked like he was about to hide behind his chair, which seemed odd. They'd gone to dinner like old friends just a couple of nights ago.

"Yes," he said wearily. "I just never knew that having a real, live fan would be so exhausting. Tell her I'll just be a few more minutes."

"You got it."

I went up to greet Ana and was taken aback again at how similar her look was to my mom's. I knew my mom dressed classically, but there was something about the way they each wore that style. Her hair was even done in the classic chignon my mom favored.

"Hello, Ana," I said, walking up to the front. Megan had just checked her in. Ana stood up from the couch, reaching out to shake my hand. Even though her shake wasn't firm, I clasped her hand back. Mom always said a firm handshake said a hundred things about a person, all of them good.

"Mickey," she said. "Aren't you quite the professional. Don't tell me your mother has you working here every day?"

"I wish," I said. "Just a couple of days a week. Giancarlo is finishing up with a client—he'll just be a few minutes. Can I get you anything while you wait?"

The usual response was somewhere along the lines of, "Could I get an iced tea or bottle of water?" Instead, Ana asked, "How about a tour?"

"A tour?" I said, a bit thrown. "Of the salon?"

"Sure, why not?" she replied. "I read all about the renovations on the blog. I'm curious to see how that basement looks. Maybe I'll book a massage while we're at it."

It's not like showing clients around the salon wasn't allowed. Plus, like Ana implied, maybe it was good business to show her the other services we offered.

"Sure," I said. "Right this way."

Ana followed me across the floor. "So, this is the main floor," I said. She walked much more slowly than I did, really looking over each of the stylists as she passed. Devon, being a bit snarky and suspicious by nature, cut her a look. Ana smiled back.

"Fantastic style," she told Devon, looking down at her 1940s military-style black dress, brass buttons and all. Devon forced a smile across her matte, red lips in response.

"Back here is the way to The Underground," I said. "That's what we call our basement."

"The Underground?" she asked. "Interesting. What made you call it that?"

"It was Cecilia—Cecilia von Tressell, from the show. She thought it sounded more exciting than just a basement."

"So it's simply a euphemism?"

"A what?"

"Never mind," she said, waving the comment off. "Let's see what happens down there."

Before we could get to the stairs, we passed the door to the storage area. "What's this here?" she asked. She stood by the product wall, looking over the bottles.

"Those are just our extra products. This is a storage area now. Also used as a break room."

She ran her eyes carefully over the shelves as if memorizing each item. I wondered what the big fascination was. I waited a moment and then finally said, "Right down here is The Underground."

She tore her eyes from the shelf, flashed a smile, and followed me down.

"This is our pedicure station, obviously," I said, pointing out the pedicure chairs on the side. "Manicures over here. Hey, Karen," I said to our head manicurist, who was working on a client.

"Hey, Mickey," she said, looking up at me.

"Hello," Ana said. "Karen? I'm Ana. Nice to meet you."

"Oh, um, this is Ana," I explained to Karen, who gave us a curious look. "She's here to see Giancarlo."

"Well, he's fantastic," Karen said. "You're in good hands."

"Don't I know it. That's all I've heard!" Ana clasped her hands to her chest like an excited little girl. "I can't wait!"

"So," I said, steering her away from Karen. "The facial area is right over here." Ana peered inside the little room as best she could even though the door was mostly closed for privacy.

"It really is quite nice down here," she said as we

headed back to the stairs. "Very relaxing and upscale. That's hard to do with a subterranean space."

"Yep," I said, because I didn't know what else to say. I was getting a little weirded out by Ana—like she was judging us but trying to be complimentary at the same time. When we got upstairs I was relieved to see Giancarlo was ready for her.

"Thanks, girl," he said after I showed her to the changing room with a robe. "I owe you."

"It was fine. She seemed really interested," I said. "If we get this reaction once the show airs, we'll be slammed every week."

When Ana hadn't come back out after a couple of minutes he said, "What's taking her so long?"

"Should I go back and check on her?" I asked.

"Maybe. I don't want her wandering off."

Why did he seem so annoyed with her when she clearly thought he was fabulous? I stepped closer to him and said, "Is there a story here?"

Giancarlo quickly shook his head. "None at all," he said emphatically.

"Okay," I said, stepping back. "Just asking."

When I went back to check on Ana in the changing rooms, she walked out from the storage area.

"Mickey!" she said, seeing me. "I'm sorry. I just got a little turned around."

"That's okay," I said, starting to wonder if it really

was. She was the nosiest customer we'd had that I could remember. "Giancarlo is ready for you."

"Great! Better show me the way up," she said. "I might get lost again!"

Ana got settled into the chair, and I sat on the stool near Giancarlo's station.

"Mickey here is helping me out today," Giancarlo told her. "I hope that's okay."

"Of course," she said. "A little Giancarlo in the making."

I couldn't help but blush—I hoped to be as good as Giancarlo someday!

"So what are we doing today?" Giancarlo asked, combing his fingers through her hair to get a feel for it. "Color touch-up, right?"

"Yes," Ana said, looking in the mirror at her own dark-brown hair.

"Want to just cover up these roots?" Giancarlo asked. Ana's roots were a lighter brown than the rest of her hair.

"Actually," she said, "I'm thinking about keeping that root color and blending the rest of my hair to it."

"Is this your natural color?" he asked.

Ana laughed a very hoity-toity laugh. "Oh, dear! Just ask me my age next!"

"Well, I need to know so I don't damage your hair," he said with a smile, keeping his professional manner.

"I assure you, I have just as much if not more experience as you with color. I just want a simple blending job, that's all."

"I'm sure you know your hair better than I do," Giancarlo said, "but I do have to point out that it's more than a simple blending—it's an all-over change. Are you absolutely sure you want to go with this color?" He looked closely at her roots again. "I'm just a little concerned it'll make your hair brittle."

"Yes, well," Ana said calmly. "I'm not going to ask you again."

With that, Giancarlo stopped inspecting her hair and looked at her in the mirror. A few of us who were within earshot did the same because it was like, *Wow, lady.*

Giancarlo forced a smile and said, "Whatever you want."

With that I decided that a quick sweep of the floor was needed. Something was happening and I wasn't sure I wanted to be around to see it. Also, I thought it might be best to stay out of Ana's line of fire. Giancarlo's, too.

The rest of Ana's appointment went pretty smoothly. As Giancarlo worked her hair, they chatted easily about new style trends. A little later, though, when Ana was in the foils under the dryer, Giancarlo came by and told her, "Time's up. Better get those foils out."

"I think it needs a tad longer," Ana said. She lifted her magazine up in front of her face.

"No," he said firmly. "It's definitely time."

"Let me just finish this article," Ana said. "Then it'll be time."

"Ana, I'm telling you," he said, not budging from his spot. "It's time to come out of those foils."

She ignored him, just kept her eyes on her magazine, her crossed leg swinging.

Giancarlo threw up his hands and muttered, "Whatever you say."

He turned and almost slammed into me. "Mickey!" he said, steadying us both by holding my shoulders. "Where is your mother?"

"On a call in her office."

He looked over at her closed door, then stormed back to his station, hastily cleaning it up. The other stylists kept one eye on him, the other on their own clients to make sure they weren't bothered by what was clearly about to become a showdown.

Finally, Ana put down her magazine and let Giancarlo lead her back to his station. That was when the real beauty nightmare began. "What? This is . . ." Ana gasped at her reflection in the mirror as Giancarlo took out the foils and the new color began to show itself. "I said I wanted you to *blend* my color, not make me look like a kid experimenting with finger paints." She clutched at the dangling, reddish-brown strands, a huge difference from the rich, dark color she'd come in with. It looked brassy and brittle.

"I tried to tell you," Giancarlo said, his brow furrowed in frustration. "Your natural color is too dark to try to make it go this light without damaging your hair."

"You're supposed to be the expert," she insisted, touching her hair. "And feel it. It's completely fried. I can't even begin to fix this now or all my hair will fall out."

"I told you to get out from beneath the dryer," Giancarlo said. He was angry, not panicking at what his client looked like. In fact, he stood there with his hands on his hips, an "I told you so" expression on his face. "You insisted on staying under too long."

"So this is my fault? Excuse me, but I did not just color my own hair. I'm sitting here in your chair, in this salon, expecting to be treated professionally."

"I don't know what to tell you, Ana," Giancarlo said. I couldn't understand why he was acting like this—there wasn't a hint of remorse in Giancarlo's voice. All he cared about in life was creating beautiful hair and he'd just done the opposite. I expected him to be mortified.

All the other clients kept turning their eyes to watch Ana freak out, even as their stylists tried to distract them. But between the bad-hair disaster and the escalating argument, it was hard not to watch.

Violet, the salon manager, rushed over to Giancarlo's station. "Is everything okay here?" she asked, giving Giancarlo a look that said it better be okay soon.

"Does it look like it's okay?" Ana spat, still holding the ends of her hair.

"I'm so sorry about this. Let's see what we can do," Violet said, her voice calm with a slight hint of panic. She combed through Ana's hair and said, "Perhaps we can strip the color out, start over."

"Are you insane?" Ana pulled her head away from Violet's hands. "And risk having my hair fall out completely? I need to speak with the owner. Right now."

In a flash, Mom was out of her office and clicking across the floor of the salon, a tight smile on her face.

"What seems to be the—Ana?"

Mom stopped short of Giancarlo's station, taking in the sight. I took it in, too. Mom knowing Ana's name, the look of utter confusion on her face, and Ana's indignant expression. What was going on?

"Hello, Chloe," Ana said, tossing her limp, brassy hair over her shoulder. She eyed herself in the mirror and said, "And here I thought you had some high-end salon, but your so-called best stylist can't do a simple color job. He's a hack."

"Whoa," I said, taking a step forward from my

spot in the back. "She did not just say that about Giancarlo."

"Slow down, girl," Devon said, gently pulling me back by my shoulder. "Stay out of it."

Suddenly I knew what it meant to be fiercely protective of a good friend. My blood boiled at such disrespect of Giancarlo.

"I didn't realize you had an appointment," Mom said to Ana, clearly confused by the situation. "I didn't even know you were in town."

"I read about Hello, Gorgeous! on *Berkshires Beauty* and thought I'd come see how you were doing. But it seems you're not doing as well as you'd like everyone to think you are." She gestured to her hair. "I wanted my color blended, and I got this hideous color. You haven't changed a bit since beauty school, Chloe. Still out to make people think you're perfect."

"Wait a minute," Mom said. She put her hand over her eyes, trying to focus. Finally she lowered her hands to her hips, turned to Giancarlo, and said, "Back up and tell me what happened."

Giancarlo stared openmouthed at Mom for a moment, no words coming out.

"Did she ask for her color to be blended?" Mom prompted him.

"Yes, but I told her . . . ," Giancarlo began, but he was so angry he couldn't get the rest of his words out.

Mom turned to me as if suddenly realizing I was there. I wanted to help Giancarlo, but with that familiar expression on Mom's face—the one that meant she was using all her energy not to explode on someone—all I wanted was to hide in the back. I thought she was going to ask me to explain but she must have reconsidered because she turned back to Giancarlo.

"She just told us," Mom said, her voice tight, "that she asked for her color to be blended. And this," she said, gently pulling the back of Ana's hair up to demonstrate, "is not blended into anything that I would ever want walking out of my salon. Giancarlo, her hair is severely damaged. Can't you see that?"

"I can," Giancarlo admitted. "I advised her against the color she asked for."

"Stop blaming your client," Ana said.

"I'm not." Giancarlo sighed, defeated. "Look, I'm sorry," he said. I felt crushed seeing him like this. I knew what it was like to be on the receiving end of one of Mom's punishments. This was not good.

Mom nodded, her disappointment clear on her face. "Ana," she said. "I'm so sorry about this. Would you like me to recolor it? Or Violet can, if you prefer. I think we'll need to treat it first, give it a deep moisturizing and let it set for a couple of days."

"I know what's best, Chloe," Ana said. "You may

have graduated first in our class, but I was right there behind you. My salon in Boston would certainly never make a mistake like this. I'm actually quite surprised you'd let something like this happen."

Mom stood rigid, listening to Ana, literally biting her lip before she spoke, carefully considering her words. "Would you like me to fix your hair, or Violet?"

"You can do it," Ana said. "That is, if you think you can squeeze me into your busy schedule."

"Of course," Mom said.

"I'll come back in a few days to have this corrected."

"Thank you for understanding, Ana," Mom said. "Giancarlo? Could I see you in my office, please?"

Without waiting, Mom turned on her three-inch heels and went back to her office. Giancarlo followed her, barely picking up his orange-sherbet leather shoes.

The salon was as quiet as closing time before Mom turned off the lights each evening. Violet led Ana over to her station, where she began combing through her hair, talking to her quietly about how they might repair it.

We didn't have to wait long to hear what was happening in Mom's office, though. As soon as the door closed we could hear her raised voice, the words muffled but the tone crystal clear. I started sweeping again, just for something to do. The other stylists busied themselves with their clients, but the level of noise had gone way down—everyone now spoke in hushed tones, the situation still so delicate. A woman checked in at the front desk and said to Megan, "I'm here to see Giancarlo?"

Megan tried to put on her best perky face and stuttered, "It'll be, uh . . . just a few . . . let me see what's . . ."

Moments later, Giancarlo came out of Mom's office. His broad, round figure was utterly slumped, and his face, usually so full of life and energy, was blank. He walked past me without a word, heading into the back. He cleared out his cubby, dumping supplies and some photos into a bag, and started out the front.

"Giancarlo . . . ?" I said. I felt like I yelled his name, but really it came out as a squeak.

He stopped by his station and grabbed his stylists' kit, quickly packing away his scissors and good comb and brush. Without looking at any of us, not even the confused client at reception, he zipped up the bag and walked out of the salon.

CHAPTER 14

As soon as Giancarlo went out the door, I went flying after him.

"Giancarlo, wait!" I called, chasing him past the shops on Camden Way, ignoring the curious looks of passersby who dodged out of my way.

He stopped abruptly and turned back to me. "Mickey, honey," he said, the anguish clear on his face. Also the anger and frustration—his face was bright red. "I need some time, okay? This is more complicated than you know. Grown-up stuff. I hate even saying that to you but—it's true. Okay?"

"You can't be leaving," I said, not hearing him. All I kept thinking was, *He can't leave.*

"It's going to be okay," he said, much calmer now. He looked closely at me and said it again: "It's going to be okay."

Every ounce of my body filled with confusion,

frustration, and even anger. What had just happened? Who was Ana? How could my mom possibly fire the best stylist at Hello, Gorgeous!?

"Mom, you can't be serious," I said, choking back a cry once we were home later that night. I had only gone back to the salon long enough to grab my bag and run back out the door. No way could I stay there without Giancarlo. "Dad, tell her!"

"Mickey, calm down," Dad said.

"And what have I told you about getting into my business," Mom snapped back at me. "You have no say in this, young lady."

"Chloe, calm down," Dad said, literally standing between us in the living room as we both overheated.

"Dad, she *fired* him," I said. "Over one mistake!"

"One mistake that could cost me my entire business," Mom said. "Mikaela, haven't you learned by now just how quickly word travels in the salon world? Everyone knows about the show I did and it hasn't even aired yet—that's how fast it travels. So to have a well-known owner come in from Boston and have an incorrect color job done—something not even close to what she asked for—could very negatively affect my business. Not to mention she could sue us in small claims court for the damage to her hair."

"If she's such a well-known salon owner, shouldn't she have known she was making a huge mistake with that color?" I argued. "Shouldn't she have known she was under the dryer for too long?"

"Do not sass me, young lady."

"I'm just saying you didn't even give him a chance to explain or to fix this. Even Devon got probation that one time."

"That was different, and besides, Giancarlo knows better. I have to say," Mom said, "that I am not surprised. Giancarlo's ego has been climbing all week. With every new appointment he got thanks to that blogpost his chest puffed up a little more. To be honest, it was ridiculous."

"He was just excited!" I said. "He deserved all those new clients. You should have been proud of him and the business he was bringing in."

"Excellent work is *expected*, not rewarded," Mom said to me, a line I'd heard from her before. "Giancarlo is no better than any of my other stylists."

"He is so," I muttered.

"Watch your tone, Mickey," Dad warned.

I slumped down onto the couch. "Who is this Ana, anyway? Why are you protecting her so much?" I asked, because she certainly had Mom on high alert like no one else I'd ever seen—not even Cecilia von Tressell.

Mom sat down in the chair by the couch, resting her head back for a moment.

Dad sat on the end of the couch near Mom. He reached for her hand and said, "I haven't heard her name in years."

"It pops up now and then in the trades," Mom said. "Two years ago she made Boston's Best Of List for hair salons." Mom looked at me and said, "We went to beauty school together. We used to be very good friends."

"Used to be?" I said. "So what, now she's jealous of you?"

"Not necessarily," Mom said. "We were very close, best friends through school. We made each other better, really pushed and supported each other. We'd help each other with assignments, give each other feedback, stay after class to do extra work. In the end we were neck and neck for graduating at the top of the class. Then something happened." Mom paused, thinking.

"What was it?" I pressed.

"As graduation neared, some salon owners from the region came in to scout us—you know, see if they wanted to offer any of us an apprenticeship. Everyone wanted one. Some of the best salons in the country are in this area. I got the biggest offer in class. I knew that made a lot of my classmates angry, but

I was so excited to go work for this world-renowned salon. I guess I thought Ana would be happy for me. Once school ended, I started work, and she moved back to Cambridge for a while." Mom shrugged. "I tried to keep in touch, but she never responded to any of my calls or e-mails. I thought she was just busy like I was."

I tried to picture Jonah or Eve being bitter about a success of mine, so bitter that they wouldn't talk to me. Honestly, though, I couldn't imagine they'd ever do that. Good friends supported each other, right? I thought of my lame attempts to talk to Eve and wondered if I'd been going about it all the wrong way.

"I guess I got so caught up in my career," Mom continued, "and my goal of opening my own salon that I didn't think much about it."

"You tried, honey," Dad said soothingly. "It takes two to keep up a friendship."

"I know," Mom said. She stared down at the floor, her gaze unfocused. "I can't believe she's here. I can't believe she came into my salon. Why wouldn't she tell me? Why wouldn't she even come say hello?"

Dad rubbed her forearm reassuringly. Mom rubbed her eyes, taking in a slow, deep breath. Finally she said, "I'm sorry, Mickey, but Giancarlo broke a major rule in the hairstyling business. He didn't do what was best for his client. It's our job to guide them toward better decisions. It's not our job to do something we know will damage someone's hair. He bent to what his client wanted knowing it would look terrible—and possibly be damaging."

Mom pushed herself up from the chair and smoothed down her skirt. "Don't worry too much, Mickey," she said. "Giancarlo is a great stylist, and it does pain me to see him go. But as talented as he is, he'll find another job in no time."

"So that's it?" I said, my voice cracking. "He's out, just like that?"

"No, honey, not just like that," she said. "He knew the decisions he was making when he worked on her hair. Now he has to deal with those consequences."

I didn't know what else to say. Giancarlo couldn't be out—it was too hard to accept.

"Can I have his phone number or e-mail?" I asked Mom. I wanted to contact him and tell him I was sorry and that he got a totally raw deal.

"I'm not sure that's a good idea, Mickey," Mom said. "At least not right now. Let's give it some time first. Okay?"

It wasn't okay, but I said, "Fine."

To Dad she said, "Should we order in tonight? It's been a long day."

"Sure," he said, standing up with her. "I'll get the menus out."

I sat on the couch while they went to the kitchen. I couldn't remember a day when I'd felt so bad. Giancarlo couldn't leave the salon. Who would help me with my boy and friend problems now? Who would style Eve's hair for the dance on Friday? Who would make me smile each day at the salon with their crazy outfits? I suddenly realized just how much Giancarlo meant to me. He helped keep me sane and made me feel special. He was my friend.

I had to agree with Mom that Giancarlo's ego had been the tiniest bit inflated, for a little while at least, but I wasn't sure that meant he hadn't paid attention to a client. I thought about Ana and how she'd acted at the salon. I didn't know much, but I knew what I felt—and I felt like something wasn't quite right.

CHAPTER 15

"Your face doesn't look good," Jonah said as I walked into his living room. I'd let myself in the back door after I pretended to eat dinner with Mom and Dad.

"Real nice," I said, plopping down on the other end of the couch. "You know how to make a girl feel great."

"I didn't mean it like that," he said. "I just mean you look upset."

"I am upset," I said.

"What happened?" he asked. He even turned down the volume on the TV. He had on the singing competition show. I guess he wanted to see the results and if the contestant he'd voted for was still in.

"It's Giancarlo," I said, leaning my head back on the sofa. "He got fired."

"Come on," Jonah said with a laugh. "He did not."

"He did," I said, and the fact that Jonah didn't

believe me for even one single second proved how ridiculous it was. I told him the whole story about Ana and what happened at home. "Mom said his arrogance was what caused the mistake on Ana's hair and that she can't tolerate sloppiness like that."

"So she fired him," Jonah said, "just like that? I can't believe it."

"I know. But it's really weird, knowing Mom knows Ana from, like, this past life. They used to be really good friends."

"I guess not anymore, huh?" he said.

"Hardly. Ana freaked out over the whole hair thing. I've never seen anyone that mad before."

"Giancarlo must have been freaked out, too," Jonah said.

"He was stunned into silence," I said. "And he's not someone who's *ever* silent." I remembered the scene, then thought of seeing them at The Kitchen earlier that week. "It's strange," I began.

"What?"

"I saw them earlier this week—Giancarlo and Ana. Kyle and I had gone for a walk and we ran into them as they were coming out of a restaurant. They acted kind of weird, especially Giancarlo. Like I had busted him doing something wrong."

"Like what?" Jonah asked.

"I don't know," I said. "But I'm starting to think

there's more to it than just dinner."

When I spotted Kyle coming toward me at school the next day, a buzz filled my belly and I had to stop myself from skipping toward him. He gave me a sunny smile, returning my own. Finally, a happy mood returned.

"Hey, how's it going?" he asked, turning to walk with me.

"Great." Clearly I was trying to forget about all the bad stuff that was happening at the salon. But it was hard not to think about it. "Mostly great, anyway," I admitted.

"Everything okay?" he asked. It made me feel good knowing how much he really cared. I could tell by the way his brown eyes looked into mine.

"Yeah," I said. "Drama at work. Drama at school." I smiled to show him it would be okay. I hoped. "Typical stuff."

"If you need anything, just let me know. 'Kay?"

"You got it," I said.

"Excited about the dance?" he asked, turning his head just so, enough to look the slightest bit unsure and unbelievably adorable. He bit his lower lip and eyed my own lips . . .

"Yeah. Totally excited," I said as we got to my

locker and I quickly spun the combo.

He leaned his shoulder against the locker next to mine. "Me too."

I got the books I needed and tossed in the ones I didn't. The whole time he just stood and watched me, a satisfied little look on his face. It made me uncomfortable and happy at the same time.

I closed my locker and instead of pushing off to walk with me, he stayed there looking at me. I stood still, just looking at him and blushing under his gaze.

"What?" I finally said.

"Nothing," he said. "Just . . ."

He leaned in toward me, a bit puckered up, his face headed straight for my face. *Here? In the hall? In front of everyone?*

In a flash I turned my head and his lips ended up in my hair by my ear.

"Oh my gosh, I'm so sorry," I said, mortified. I touched the spot where his face planted.

"No, um, it's cool," Kyle said, straightening up and backing away from me a little. "Your, uh, hair smells good."

"Thanks," I said, trying to regain what little composure I had left. "It better, considering who my mom is. Are you, um, okay?"

"Of course. And if anyone ever asks, your hair tastes like mangoes." I laughed an embarrassed laugh as we finally started down the hall together.

Oh my god. He had totally tried to kiss me. In the hall. At school!

Did that really just happen? Was he trying to kiss me in public? If nothing else, I was pretty sure that was against school policy.

"Are you okay?" Kyle asked. "You've been a bit edgy lately."

"Just stressed—about Eve and this stuff that's happening at the salon," I said. I focused on the hall ahead, trying to avoid looking him in the eyes.

I suddenly felt overwhelmed. Kyle wanted to kiss me and I didn't know if I was ready. I wanted to help Giancarlo but I didn't know how. I still didn't know if Jonah and Eve (and Marla?) were going to the dance tomorrow. Everything was still up in the air because of Eve's project and Marla being in town. She was always around . . .

Suddenly I had an idea that could help Eve and me. And it all had to do with Marla.

"Hey, Eve!" I said, catching up with her in the hallway. "Got a sec?"

"Um, yeah, sure," she said.

I walked with her, even though it was the opposite direction of where I needed to go. "I was thinking

159

about your project for science."

She grabbed my arm. "Please tell me you have an idea."

"Well, not exactly," I said, patting her hand but really wanting to pry it off my arm. The girl had strength. "But maybe something that'll help you figure it out."

She let go and dropped her arm by her side. "There's nothing to figure out. I just need an idea."

"That's why you're going to the Feigenbaum Hall of Innovation," I said as if I were giving her tickets to Six Flags. "You can go there after school and get inspired!"

Her body slumped over the books she held in her arms. "That's actually really nice, Mickey. But Marla's here. I can't just leave her. She likes hanging out with her aunt and cousins and all but by four o'clock she's about hit capacity for family togetherness. I can't ditch her after school, too. And as I learned the hard way, she's not exactly a museum kind of girl."

"You won't have to worry about her," I said. "Because she can come with me after school!"

Eve looked at me sideways. "Come with you where?"

"Just to the mall for a little shopping. Kristen and Lizbeth will be there, too," I said. "She does like to go shopping, doesn't she?" Because if she didn't, the girl was not human.

"She loves shopping," Eve said, and I breathed a sigh of relief. "But . . . I don't know."

"About what?" I asked. Maybe I knew, but I hoped it wasn't what I thought.

"I should call Marla first and see what plans she has."

"Sure," I said.

Eve got out her phone right there in the hall and started calling. We moved to the side and leaned against the wall. *See what plans she has*—sure. I could understand Eve's hesitation. It's not like Marla and I had exactly hit it off. But I hoped she saw the free time to focus on her project as more important than worrying about me and Marla. I could—and would—put my loyalty to Eve above my not-so-great-feelings about Marla.

"Hey," Eve said into her phone. "It's me. Listen, you know that science project that's been killing me this week? I have to finish it tonight so I was wondering—do you want to hang out with Mickey tonight? Do some shopping while I work on it?" I inspected my nails and pretended not to be listening as I strained my ears to hear every word. "No, Kristen and Lizbeth will be there, too." Eve angled her body slightly away from me. "It's just for a couple of hours. You said you needed a new dress for the dance, anyway. You might have some fun. Fine, I owe you."

I all of a sudden wished I couldn't hear Eve. I backed away a little.

She finally ended the call and turned back to me. "All set! She'll meet us here after school and then I'll go to the museum and you guys can go to the mall."

"Cool," I said. "Did you say she's going to the dance on Friday?"

"Yeah, I convinced her that I wouldn't leave her alone in a corner and we'd all have fun together."

"Yeah," I said. "Fun."

"So we're all set then," she said. "For after school?"

"Yep," I said, feeling the knots tighten in my stomach. "All set."

What had I gotten myself into this time?

CHAPTER 16

"Mickey, this is a great idea," Kristen said as we waited for Marla to meet us after school.

"I hope it's okay," I said, keeping a careful watch on the road for her arrival. I was nervous, having no idea how this whole thing would go.

"It's going to be fine," Lizbeth said, reassuring me. "There's nothing to be nervous about."

"I'm not nervous," I said, totally lying.

"We're all here together," Lizbeth said. "Supporting each other, all for the good of Eve. Besides, nothing bad ever happens at the mall."

"Hi," a voice behind us said.

We turned back toward the school and saw Marla standing there wearing large sunglasses that fit her face perfectly.

"Hey, Marla," I said, quickly changing my tone. "We didn't know you were here already. Were you inside the school?" Because otherwise she'd just managed a total ninja sneak attack.

"I had to turn in a signed form to go to the dance," she said.

"We're so excited you're going," Lizbeth said. I told them she was in for the dance when I brought them up to date about my shopping idea.

"Yeah," Marla said. "Should be cool."

It was impossible to read her expression from behind those sunglasses, but I couldn't tell if she really was excited about it or if she wanted no part of it.

"Ready to head over to the mall?" I asked.

"Sure," Kristen said.

"Great," Lizbeth said.

"I guess," Marla said.

Yep. She wanted no part of it at all. Great. This was going to be a long—I mean, *interesting*—afternoon.

Once we got to the mall, I felt like I was the one who had to be in charge. Kristen and Lizbeth seemed to be watching me and Marla to see what might happen, like we were a reality show they couldn't turn away from. As for Marla herself, she walked a little ahead of us as if she knew where she was going—even though this was our town.

"So," I said, "the goal is dresses for tomorrow night. And whatever else you want to look at, like accessories. Also, I have a genius strategy for mall shopping. It's all about where you start. The key is, it doesn't have to be at the end here. It can be in the middle or at the other end. You just have to know where you're going next."

"Great plan," Lizbeth said.

"Um, that's actually my plan," Marla said. "Eve and I came up with it."

"Oh," I said. Why was she being so defensive about it? I tried to stay calm and shrug it off. I wasn't about to start something with her. "That makes sense. I mean, I learned it from Eve so . . . it's a genius plan."

"Thanks," Marla said. "We came up with it together when we were, like, nine."

"Okay. Cool," I said. There was something about the way she insisted on letting me know it was *her* idea that made me wish I hadn't brought it up in the first place.

"So!" Lizbeth jumped in to rescue me. "Where should we start? I think maybe Monahan's is having a sale."

"Sounds good to me," Kristen said, shooting me a look. Had I done something wrong? I was trying my best here!

We started toward the store and I said, "I have another idea for Eve. Since she has to work on her project tonight, maybe we can look for a dress for her, too. We can pull a few and put them on hold, maybe even take pictures of them so she can decide without having to come here. That way she can come by tomorrow after school and just snag the one she wants. It'll be a tight turnaround and she may not even have time, but I thought it might be nice, just in case."

"That's a great idea, Mickey," Lizbeth said.

"If we're doing that then we might as well skip Monahan's," Marla said. "Totally not Eve's style."

"Oh, well, it's just in case," I said, trying really hard to maintain cool. "And Monahan's has a ton of styles. I'm sure we can find something."

"If you think so." Marla smiled, but it wasn't a friendly smile. I was getting the feeling that no matter how hard I worked, Marla wasn't about to give me an inch.

"How about we go to the department store down here," Lizbeth said. "There are all kinds of dresses. I'm sure we can find something for all of us."

We started in that direction, and I took the moment to calm myself. I was not in a competition with Marla, but I felt like maybe she was forcing me into one. I could be nice and not aggressive. I could do it for Eve. What Marla wanted to do was up to her.

"Marla," Kristen said. "Are you excited about going to the dance?"

Marla pulled her white fringe bag up higher on her shoulder. "I guess. I'm kind of afraid to talk much more about it to Eve, to be honest. She's been pretty stressed all week about this project."

Wow, I thought. *Emotions!*

Okay, that was mean.

To her, I said, "It's going to be so much fun. We'll all hang out together."

"Well, she does have a boyfriend," she said as if I were stupid for forgetting. "She'll probably want to spend some time with him."

"I know," I said. "He's my best friend."

"I thought *Eve* was your best friend?" Marla said, and it felt like a challenge. Like she was just trying to stick me where it hurt.

"I think the party dresses are on the second floor," Lizbeth said before I could respond.

We got to the dress section and Marla immediately branched off and started flipping through the racks.

"You okay?" Lizbeth asked.

I glanced over at Marla. She held out an apricot dress that I seriously hoped she wasn't considering for Eve.

"Is it just me or is she trying to make it hard for me?" I tried to concentrate on the dresses, but I was too distracted. "That whole 'I thought Eve was your best friend' comment—what was that?"

"It was really harsh," Lizbeth agreed. "You're a champ for trying but maybe you two just aren't going to be friends."

"That's putting it lightly," I said.

"You're trying, you're being nice, and if she can't accept that then what else can you do?"

"But I promised Eve I'd take care of her," I said.

"And you are," Lizbeth said. She pulled out a draped green dress. "But it doesn't mean you have to put up with her snotty comments."

"True," I said. I looked back to Marla, who thumbed intently through a new rack of dresses. "I still want to try, though."

"You're very brave," Lizbeth said, putting the green dress back. "Good luck."

I walked over to where Marla stood looking at more dresses. She had a lemon-yellow number thrown over her shoulder.

"Find anything good?" I asked, looking to the hideously colored dress.

"Just this one," she said. She held it out—high asymmetrical neck, cap sleeves, medium length. Horrendous.

"For Eve?"

"Yeah," she said, slinging it back over her shoulder. "It'll really work with her coloring."

"You think?" I asked about the electric-yellow dress. "It's a hard color to pull off."

"And if anyone can do it, Eve can," she said. She moved over to a new rack of clothes, and I casually followed her.

"I was thinking of surprising her with a styling session at my mom's salon tomorrow," I said, pressing forward. I wasn't sure what was happening at the salon with GC gone, and frankly, I didn't want to think about it. But I'd already told Eve about it, so I was leaving the invitation open. "Give her some big, dramatic curls."

Marla wrinkled her nose. "Eve with curls? She'd hate that."

I stopped pretending to look through the racks with Marla and said, "I don't think she would."

"It would look terrible on her."

"Um, excuse me," I said, because I don't even think so. This was *hair* she was talking about. "First of all, Eve would look amazing with curls. If anyone could pull them off, it's her."

Marla paused long enough to glare at me.

"Second, we only have the best stylists in the country at our salon, and they could make anyone look incredible in just about any style. So please don't question what Eve might look like once they're done with her, okay? Because she will look amazing."

"Fine, calm down," Marla said as if *I* were the one who was being a pain. From the corner of my eye I could see Kristen and Lizbeth shuffling toward us through the racks. "I'm just saying, I'm not sure if *curls* are her thing."

"What's wrong with curls?" I asked, because hello! I am curl-centric!

She sighed as if this whole conversation were totally annoying. But she started it. "Nothing is wrong with them. They're just not my thing. Don't take it personally. It's not a character assassination or anything. Sheesh."

"Fine," I said. "I mean, I happen to think Eve could pull just about any look off because she's so pretty, but if you don't think so we could tell her."

She turned to me and said, "You know that's not what I'm saying, okay?"

"Yeah, sure," I said, my face heating up. "Fine."

"Look, *Mickey*," she said, saying my name with a sneer.

"Guys!" Lizbeth said, finally arriving at our racks with Kristen. "Calm down, okay?"

"Yeah," Kristen said. "Don't kill each other. Juvie's not worth it."

"Kristen . . ." Lizbeth sighed.

"What? I'm trying to lighten the situation."

"I'm just saying," Marla continued, ignoring Kristen and Lizbeth, "it's actually not personal, okay? I'm just looking out for Eve. I can't be cool with someone who isn't cool with my friend."

"I'm looking out for Eve, too!" I said, raising my voice. Just what did she think we were doing there? And who was *she*, anyway? Eve's personal bodyguard?

"You guys," Lizbeth said. "Seriously. Calm down."

"If you were looking out for Eve," Marla said, "you wouldn't have done what you did."

"You don't know anything about our friendship," I said.

"Truce!" Kristen said. "Someone call it! Security will be here any second!"

I didn't know if she was serious about security or not, but I did take a breath and a step back. Marla folded her arms over her chest and I just waited for her to say "She started it."

"Fine," I said. I waited for Marla to say something similar, but she didn't. She began pawing through the racks again as if the whole thing were over. But it so wasn't. I had to remember the truth of what I'd just said—we were there for Eve. "Marla, listen." I took a deep breath. "This is so dumb. We are here for Eve. Both of us. Right?"

"Of course," she said.

"I'm trying to make things up to Eve. But that's between us. She's an awesome person who deserves a big night of fun in a pretty dress, especially after how hard she's been working on this project. I just want to make sure we find that for her. All right?"

Her face softened. "Right."

"I know there are, like, fifty dresses here that would look amazing on Eve. So let's find her a few options, send her pics, and put them on hold. Okay?"

"Definitely," she said. "And just so you know, I don't hate you. I know Eve can look out for herself." She paused, staring at her shoes for a minute. Finally, she looked up at me, her eyes a little sad. "It's just weird seeing her with all her new friends after not being around her every day anymore. I've missed her since she left. That's all."

Eve and I had talked about how hard it was for her to move away from her friends, even though it wasn't that far. At the time she said she didn't want to be all whiny about it, and I told her that if it were me I'd be whining all day long. She made it look so easy that it was hard to imagine she wasn't anything other than self-assured and outgoing. But I bet she felt a lot like Marla did now. A lot like I'd been feeling in the past week. Without a best friend—someone you just clicked with—it was easy to feel entirely alone.

"So, should we truce?" I asked, offering my hand.

Marla looked at it for a moment, then smiled and said, "Of course. For Eve—and because I *suppose* you're not horrible."

"Ha-ha," I said. "Not funny."

Okay, maybe we weren't going to be best friends, but we could join forces.

And we did. As we pushed through more racks, looking for the perfect dress for Eve, Marla and I both emerged with our favorite choices. She held up a pale-pink number, and I had picked out a royal-blue one.

"That's pretty cute," Marla said, a hint of surprise in her voice.

"So's that one," I said of the spaghetti-strapped dress with a belted waist. "That cut would look really cute on Eve."

Marla held the dress aloft and headed through the racks to me. "That one, too. She loves wearing bold colors."

I looked at the dress more closely. "The only thing I'm worried about is the length—it's a bit long, like it'll come just below her knee."

"Hmm, you may be right," Marla said, holding out the end of the dress. "She'd have to have it altered."

"And there's no time for that."

"Not to mention she'd have to spend more money on it," Marla said.

"True." I looked at the pale-pink dress she'd picked out once again. "This is really cute. I think Eve would like it. Want to take a pic to send to her, then put it on hold in case she wants it?"

"Sounds good," Marla said. "And if we find others we'll do the same."

"Agreed," I said.

We found a couple more and took their pics as well.

More importantly, though, was that Marla and I hadn't killed each other in the process. For that alone Eve would be happy. I just hoped she had time to choose a dress—maybe even one of the dresses we'd picked out.

It seemed like everything lately hung on by a tiny thread of time. I wondered how it would all work out.

CHAPTER 17

Once we left the mall, I wanted to go to the salon—usually the place I could calm down and feel more like myself. However, I knew things were bleak there with Giancarlo gone. I wasn't even sure I wanted to be there without him, but I decided to see if Mom had finally come to her senses and rehired him.

When I walked in the doors I immediately felt the change. The salon felt quieter. Don't get me wrong, business was booming, but that magic buzz was missing.

"Hey, Megan," I said, walking up to the reception desk.

She smiled, but it wasn't the big, happy smile she usually gave. It was something more reserved. "Hi, Mickey. What brings you by?"

"I don't know," I said, looking at Giancarlo's empty station and feeling a pull in the pit of my stomach. This wasn't right at all. "It's quiet here, isn't it?"

Megan looked back out at the salon, taking in the stylists working on their clients. But she nodded her head and said, "It's definitely been a bit quiet." I thought she was going to say "since Giancarlo left," but she didn't. "The truth is, I think everyone is a bit gun-shy. I've seen stylists fired, but never like that. And *never* someone like Giancarlo."

"I don't think he should have been fired," I said. Megan didn't say anything to that. Might have been that whole gun-shy thing and the fact that Mom was her boss. "Want me to bring you up a drink or anything?"

"Nah," she said. "Thanks, though, Mickey."

I found Mom in her office, going through her e-mails.

"Have fun at the mall, sweetie?" she asked, glancing up at me between typing.

"Yeah," I said. "A little dramatic but good in the end."

"Drama—ugh," she said. "The last thing I need more of."

"Mom, can I ask you something?"

"Sure, honey," she said, keeping her eyes on her computer.

"About Giancarlo," I said.

"Mickey," Mom said, looking at me. "I am not going to get into that." She sat back in her chair.

"Come here," she said, reaching her hand out to me. I walked over and stood beside her desk. I let her hold my hand, even though I felt like I wasn't going to like what was coming. "I know how you feel about Giancarlo. And he was—is—a wonderful stylist. One of the best I've ever had. He's going to be fine—I promise. This is just business."

"Yeah, but maybe the whole thing was Ana's fault. Maybe Giancarlo was right all along."

"Mickey, I would think Ana knows how to properly ask a stylist for what she wants—and Giancarlo should have been able to do that. I know clients sometimes ask for one thing and get something that they didn't quite picture—we can't read people's minds. But this was entirely different. I think you know that."

I didn't know that, but I didn't say anything. There'd been something about Ana all along that I couldn't quite put my finger on. I wasn't about to give up, though. Not on Giancarlo, not ever.

"Do you mind if I stay? Do my homework in the back?" I asked. The truth was, I hardly had any homework, but I needed to do some investigating about what truly happened with Giancarlo and Ana.

"Can you concentrate here?" she asked.

"Yeah," I said. "Besides, I don't have much to do."

"Okay, then," she said. With Mom working in her

office, I knew it was unlikely she'd come to the back. I'd be in the clear.

I went back to the storage room and, in about fifteen minutes, finished the short English worksheet I had shoved in my bag. Then I went to look at the inventory. I grabbed the clipboard that listed the products—shampoo, conditioner, mousses, gels, pomades, setting lotions, silicone sprays, and of course the hair colors.

On a small section of the wall hung the color chart, with little samples of fake hair to show what the color would look like. Beneath the little curl of hair was the name, like Sable Lux, Shy-Dye Blond, and Rita Red. Numbers corresponded to those colors that matched the bottles on the shelves. We took inventory once a week to see what color was used the most and reordered more of that than the others. In short, the chart should show exactly what colors were used that week. All I'd have to do is ask the stylists what they used, compare that to the chart, and make sure it all added up.

I remembered how Ana had been lingering back here by the colors when she should have been in the changing room. She'd said she'd gotten lost, but . . . I'd just given her a full tour. Something was starting to smell like a bad perm left under the dryer too long. I wondered if the inventory could be off. Maybe somehow Ana slipped in a wrong color to make her dye job go so horribly wrong? I checked the list against what was on the shelves and everything checked out. *Figures,* I thought. Besides, Giancarlo would have known the color was off as soon as he mixed it and certainly before he put it on her hair. I didn't know what I was looking for, but whatever it was I hadn't found it yet.

Devon came to the back to get some styling mousse. "Hey, Micks," she said. "What are you doing here?"

"Just dropped by after shopping," I said. Devon was always straight-up honest, so I thought I could bring up what happened without her shutting down about it. No one else seemed to want to mention Giancarlo. "Can I ask you a question?"

"Sure," she said.

"What did you think of that whole thing with Giancarlo and Ana?"

"I thought it was pretty messed up."

"Do you think it was his fault, though?"

"I can't say," Devon said. "It's a tricky area. When a client asks you to do something to their hair that's against your training and knowledge as a stylist, you have to be really careful. Your job is to please the client but also to make them look amazing. The worst thing you can do," she said, "is damage a client's hair. That's something that won't just get you fired—it could land you in court."

"That's what Mom said," I told her. "She said Ana could sue her in small claims court."

"She could, if she really thought her hair was damaged that badly and that Giancarlo was negligent. It's pretty serious stuff."

"I just don't believe it," I said. "I don't know—something about that Ana woman."

"I heard she and your mom have some sort of history?" Devon said.

"Yeah," I said. "That and some kind of big fight."

"Well, I'm sure it's just that," Devon said. "You're being protective of your mom—and Giancarlo—because of that. Try not to worry about it."

The fact that Devon wasn't buying into my convoluted theory told me that maybe I *was* overthinking it. Maybe I just didn't want to believe Giancarlo had messed up.

Later, as I rode home with Mom, I couldn't stop thinking about it all. Maybe Ana didn't secretly sabotage the color in the dish by swiping a bottle out of the back, but she did *something*. She had to have.

"When is Ana coming in to have her hair fixed?" I asked.

"Tomorrow," Mom said. She glanced at me and said, "Why?"

"I'm just thinking," I said. "What if Ana deliberately messed up her hair?"

"Mickey," Mom said, sighing. "First of all, that is ridiculous, second of all, that is impossible, and third of all—I told you to stay out of it. Don't make me tell you again. I appreciate your help at the salon, but this is adult business."

"But, Mom, you said yourself that you guys ended things badly. What if she's back for revenge?"

Mom almost laughed. "Mickey, I think you've been watching too many movies."

"But you know Giancarlo is a better stylist than anyone," I said. "No way would he ruin someone's hair."

"But he did, Mickey," Mom said. "We all saw it."

We turned onto a residential road in our neighborhood.

"You know, Giancarlo told Ana it was time to get out from under the dryer," I said. "I heard him and she refused. She said it wasn't time yet and insisted on finishing whatever article she was reading."

Mom kept a steady watch on the road. "Really?"

"Yeah," I said. "And I saw them out together the other night. Coming out of The Kitchen."

"You did? What were they doing there?"

"I don't know. But yesterday Giancarlo seemed kind of, I don't know—funny."

"Funny how?" Mom asked.

"I'm not sure. Like he was uncomfortable or something. One day they're like old friends, the next, he seemed a little . . ."

"Mickey," Mom said. "I'm not sure I can get involved in this."

"But it's Giancarlo, Mom!"

"Yes, but his having dinner with Ana the other night and Ana supposedly staying under the dryer to finish an article doesn't add up to anything. I already told you—I don't want you getting involved in this."

"Maybe it doesn't all add up yet," I said. "But isn't it enough to look at things a little more closely? Just so we can know for sure that nothing out of the ordinary has happened?"

I could see her jaw clenching in the passing light of a streetlamp. "What are you proposing?"

I shifted my body toward Mom as much as my seat belt would let me. "Ana's coming in tomorrow, right? So we just casually ask her a few questions. Conversationlike. Just to see."

"You think you can get her to admit that she purposely ruined her own hair? And what does dinner with Giancarlo have to do with anything?"

"I don't know," I said, feeling frustrated because I didn't have any of the answers. "But that's what we're going to find out."

Mom turned onto our street, passing the other white clapboard houses with perfectly manicured, green lawns. "I guess I have been thinking a lot about Giancarlo since it happened. Some part of me doesn't feel good about it, either."

"See!" I said. "So can we talk to Ana tomorrow?"

Mom turned into our driveway, pulled into the garage, and cut the engine. I sat and waited for her answer.

"I need something more concrete to go on than a dinner and an article. If you can tell me something solid, then I'll think about it," Mom said.

"Yes!"

"But it won't be some attack campaign. We'll just have a little chat with Ana. Got it?"

"Got it," I said. What I didn't say was that I'd do anything to get Giancarlo back at the salon where he belonged—especially if it meant outing the person who had hurt him.

CHAPTER 18

When I saw Eve at school the next day, I wanted to pounce and see how the museum went, if she finished her project, and what she thought of the dresses we'd texted her. But I managed to play it cool until she came up to me as I walked into the cafeteria for lunch.

"So," she said, walking beside me. "I heard about last night."

I knew immediately that she meant my fight with Marla in the midst of party dresses at the mall. "Listen, Eve, I'm really sorry—"

"Thank you so—sorry for what?" she asked, our sentences crossing. "What happened?"

"Um, nothing," I said. Was it possible Marla *didn't* tell her? "I was just going to say sorry you had to work until the last minute on your project. How'd it go?"

"Great," she said as we entered the caf together.

"The Feigenbaum was just what I needed to get a little inspiration. I came up with a solution for static electricity and hair. I got home before you guys finished at the mall and started working on my presentation. Marla helped me finish it up when she got home."

"That's great," I said. "How'd you do it?"

"We came up with a brush that could pump antistatic spray while you brush. Kind of like the stuff you can use on clothes. The brush was kind of wonky but the idea and presentation were good so—everything worked out!"

"That's amazing!" I cheered. "I'm really happy for you, Eve."

"It's all thanks to you," she said.

"And Marla," I said. "And Kristen and Lizbeth. It was a total team effort."

We sat down next to each other at the table. Jonah and Kyle weren't there yet and neither were Kristen and Lizbeth.

"Marla said you guys had a great time," Eve said.

"Really?" I asked. I know things ended well, but I wasn't convinced Marla was a big fan of mine. But it had been . . . fun. After the almost-catfight and all. "I mean, yeah, we had a good time."

"She said you have a fierce sense of style."

"Really? She said that?"

Eve nodded as she unpacked her lunch. "She also said you're a superloyal friend to me. Mickey, I know you guys had a rough start," she said, eyeing me with a little smile on her face. "Marla told me all about it. But she said it ended up being cool with you guys working it all out."

"We did," I said. "And it was. Rough, I mean. That girl will not back down."

Eve laughed. "Tell me about it. It's her best and worst quality. I think it's really sweet how both of you were just trying to look out for me. Thanks for doing that, Mickey. I really appreciate it."

I smiled. "No big deal. You'd do it for me."

I wasn't sure about that last part, but I hoped it was true. Eve didn't say anything one way or the other.

"So tell me about your project," I said. "You got it done—that's good!"

"I know," she sighed. "Now I know how you feel—always waiting until the last moment."

"A great adrenaline rush, isn't it?" I said and laughed.

"That's one way to describe it," she said. "Another way would be massive anxiety and paralyzing fear."

Kristen and Lizbeth came over and sat down across from us.

"You guys," Kristen said after we all said hello. "I'm seriously rethinking this whole going to the dance alone thing. Seems like a lot of work to make a lame guy jealous. I mean, he's not worth the trouble."

"I told you," Lizbeth said, "it's fine if you go with me and Matthew."

"And does Matthew know this?" Kristen asked.

"Not yet," Lizbeth admitted. "But I'm sure he won't mind."

"Sure," Kristen said. "There's nothing I love more than being a third wheel. I think I'll pass."

"Who's a third wheel?" Jonah asked as he and Kyle sat down, each on either side of me and Eve.

"I don't want to talk about it anymore," Kristen said.

"Not Tobias again?" Kyle said. "When are you going to give it up already?"

"I have," she said. "I'm done."

"They're done," I said to Kyle, "but Lizbeth and Matthew are fine. Eve is done with her science project, and Marla said she's cool going to our dance. So that means we'll all be there together—right, Eve?"

"Well," she said. "Truthfully, I don't think I can handle the dance tonight. I already talked to Jonah about it. After this crazy week, having a friend in town, and working on this monster project, I just want to veg out. But text me and maybe we'll meet you guys somewhere afterward."

"Are you sure?" I asked, disappointed. "Didn't you get the pictures of the dresses we texted you? It won't take any time to pop in after school and check them out."

"Thanks for sending me those, but sorry," she said. "It's been a long week. I just don't feel like it."

"Have fun, suckers," Jonah said, but I think he mainly meant that for Kyle. I didn't want to seem desperate, but I really wanted Eve to come. It would be more fun to have the whole group there. Plus I was sure it'd help our friendship if we could hang out together again. It was always more fun with all of us. I was bummed.

"I guess that just leaves us," I said to Kyle. The kiss would happen tonight, I was sure of it. My stomach fluttered at the thought. I wondered if I'd be ready.

"And that would be horrible, wouldn't it?" Kyle said, standing up from the table and grabbing his tray. "If you don't want to go . . . maybe we should talk later." He stormed off.

I was stunned. The whole table fell quiet, staring at me. I didn't know what I'd done, but I knew that while things were finally on the mend with Eve, I'd somehow just blown it with Kyle.

I couldn't find him anywhere. He hadn't gotten that much of a head start but when I left the caf and started through the halls he was nowhere to be found.

I looked in an empty classroom but didn't see him. I checked the library and the gym and the hall near his locker. I sent him a text but he didn't text back. I slumped against a row of lockers, wondering what I'd done.

Class would start soon—what if I couldn't find him before the end of the day? We hadn't exactly decided where to meet tonight. Would we even still be going together? Did his storming out mean he'd just broken up with me?

My phone buzzed with a new text. "Turn around," I read. I turned. Way at the end of the hall stood Kyle, staring back at me. He nodded his head for me to follow, so I did.

He went out a side door and stopped on a sidewalk that led to the teachers' parking lot. I wasn't sure if we were supposed to be out there, but didn't say anything. The breeze blew his hair across his forehead, and although it was a little cloudy, there was a brightness to the day that made us both squint.

"Look, do you still want to go to the dance with me or what?"

"Yes!" I said. "Of course."

"Because you're acting like you don't. Do you still even like me?"

"Yes," I said again. "I do. I'm just acting crazy this week."

"Mickey, you're *always* acting crazy. Which is fine.

But this time you're acting crazy toward me. I just get this feeling that you don't want to be with me."

"No, I promise. It's not that. It's nothing."

He leaned his shoulder against the wall and put his hands in his pocket. "You sure?"

"Yes, I'm sure," I said. I did like Kyle. I wanted to go to the dance with him and hang out and talk more. "I just have a lot going on, but by the time we meet for the dance it'll all be done with and I'll be ready to just have fun."

He looked down at the sidewalk when he said, "I don't want to go as a group. Seeing everyone there is fine. But I had plans for us. So if it's okay with you, I'd rather not go as a group or double with anyone or anything. Okay?"

"Yeah, sounds good. Um, I'm getting my hair done at the salon." I thought about the stunt we were going to have to pull off to get Giancarlo his job back. I'd be cutting time pretty close. "Do you want to pick me up there? Is that okay?"

"Sure, it's fine," he said. "The dance starts at seven so maybe I'll pick you up then? At seven?"

"Perfect," I said. "We don't want to be the first ones there."

He looked at me, smiling. "Definitely not." He held my gaze for a moment before reaching out to take my hand. "Ready to go back inside?"

I took his hand, holding it lightly, comfortably. What was I so nervous about?

"Ready," I said.

CHAPTER 19

After school I sprinted out the door and headed to Hello, Gorgeous!, article in hand. If anyone asked me, I'd say the information I'd found was *shocking*.

When I got to the salon, I immediately went to Mom's office.

"I'm not sure about this," she said, pacing back and forth. "It feels a bit . . . ," she said, circling her hand in front of her, "juvenile."

"I told you, Mom—it's for Giancarlo. Besides," I said, handing her the article. "I found this."

"What is it?" she asked, looking at the printout.

"An article I found online last night from a Boston magazine."

I'd gone online after everyone went to bed. I waited until now to give it to Mom just in case I found more at school on the library computers. Truthfully, this was enough.

What began as a small but promising salon soon became the darling of Newbury Street. Appointments were booked up to six weeks in advance with the stylists catering to the elite of Boston society. No woman was ready for the weekend's gala, benefit, or special event without a visit to Ana Steiner's Hello, Beautiful. Sadly, Ms. Steiner's gem of a salon has lost its glamorous edge. Call it a case of overconfidence—or some might even say greed.

"Once she made the Boston Best Of List, she changed," former stylist Victoria Frame said. "She threw a ton of money into all these changes and renovations, hired even more stylists, and started treating some of the staff, well . . . not very nicely."

Another former staff member, who asked not to be named, said Ms. Steiner became so focused on expanding that she forgot about quality. "She even messed up the cut on one of her own clients because she kept going back and forth to the phone to talk about putting down new tile in the salon. It was pretty bad."

"The meaner she got, the more the staff slacked off," Rick, another former stylist, who asked that we only use his first name, said. "We just didn't respect her anymore, so I guess we sort of rebelled by refusing to keep the salon clean or even book her clients. Pretty soon most of us had one foot out the door, and when we left we took our clients with us." He paused, thinking.

"I felt kind of bad about that. But she kind of gave us no choice. It wasn't a good work environment."

Now, Hello, Beautiful may be closing its doors for good unless it can get the quality stylists it so desperately needs back behind the chairs. Ms. Steiner wouldn't comment for this story, but word has it that she's already three months behind on her lease and running out of time.

"It's a beautiful space, and she's been a good tenant until now," said Marilyn Owens, who owns the 1902 brownstone on Newbury Street in which Hello, Beautiful resides. "I think her salon had an identity crisis and the clients didn't feel as comfortable there as they used to. I know I don't."

It's that mentality that is sinking this once-glamorous salon. Call it a sign of these economically uncertain times—or simply a cautionary tale of letting fame go to one's well-coifed head.

Mom put the printout down and stared across her desk.

"See?" I said. "She's desperate for good stylists. Her business is in trouble so maybe she came here for ideas. She asked for a tour of the salon, I forgot to tell you that. I think it all adds up, Mom. She tried to *steal* Giancarlo away from us!"

"I'm going to give her the best salon treatment of her

life," Mom said, still staring across her desk.

"The best?" I said, confused. "She deserves the worst. We can't let her get away with it."

Mom's phone rang and she hit the speaker. "Yes?"

"Your client is here," Megan said. "Ana Steiner."

"Thanks. I'll be right up." Mom stood up from her chair. "Mickey, thank you for finding this article for me. Now let me handle what happens out there. Okay?"

"Okay," I said.

Mom and I walked out together. Ana stood at the front, leaning her hip on the counter and looking around the salon like she did last time. I still had to admit she had great style. The slim, dark denim jeans with heels and a scarf covering her hair looked like Mom's weekend outfit—sans the scarf, anyway.

I got my broom from the back to sweep around and keep an eye (and ear) on Mom and Ana, while Mom led Ana back to change into a robe. As she changed, my phone buzzed in my pocket—a text from Eve.

Changed mind. I'm in for tonight. See you at the salon for GC to style me? Ok to bring Marla?

I wasn't sure anymore about the offer to style her hair. Eve didn't know that Giancarlo was no longer a stylist here. I thought about how I could make it work. I could give Eve my slot with Mom and I could do Marla's hair if she'd let me. Then if there was time I'd do my own. It wasn't a great plan but I couldn't offer something to Eve and then take it back.

Sounds great. And yes, bring Marla. See you tonight!

Ana now sat in Mom's chair—the one closest to the front of the salon with the best view of the clients coming in and what the stylists were doing all around her.

"It's been a long time, Ana," Mom said, working her fingers through Ana's hair the way all stylists did the moment a client sat in their chair. "I didn't realize you were going to be in town. We could have had lunch, caught up."

"Truthfully," Ana said, "I didn't realize this was your salon. I was curious because of the name—very similar to my own."

Mom nodded, calm and self-assured. "When did you open your salon?"

"Seven years ago," Ana said.

"Yes, that's about when I opened mine." She smiled at Ana in the mirror—a cutting, warning kind of smile. "Let's get you washed."

"Yes, I really do need to get moving," Ana said, standing up from Mom's chair. "Rockford is very charming but these small towns start to make me claustrophobic. I really admire you for being able to stay here all these years. It's like being cut off from the real world."

I wanted to pounce in and ask Ana just who did she think she was, talking about Rockford that way. It happened to be a great town. But Mom didn't react. Just nodded along and said, "Oh, it's not as bad as you might think."

As Mom washed her hair, I noticed that she gave Ana an extra-long head massage. Ana had been talking as Mom washed her hair about how busy her salon was (lie) and joking about how many stoplights Rockford had (mean), but Mom just massaged away until finally Ana's eyes fell shut and she was quiet.

After her deep conditioning, she was back in Mom's chair, ready to have her hair colored back to whatever it was that she had supposedly originally wanted. I kept sweeping around as casually as I could, ready to jump in when Mom wanted me. But someone else came in before it was my turn to help.

Giancarlo appeared in the door, a big, hulking wonder of styling grace in clashing horizontal and vertical striped pants and shirt. I had to resist the urge to run up and hug him.

"Hello, Miss Megan," he said at the reception desk. "I hope I'm not here at a bad time."

"Of course not!" she said, and I had to admit, she didn't seem too surprised to see him.

Giancarlo angled his body toward Mom's station and said, "I'm just here to pick up my final paycheck."

"Sure, let me ask Chloe about it," Megan said. She went to Mom's station, and Mom told her, "It's on my desk in my office. You can go on back and get it."

Megan went back while Giancarlo waited at reception.

"How are you, Giancarlo?" Mom asked very casually as if he weren't someone she had fired just that week.

"Good, Chloe, I'm good," he said. "Hello, Ana."

Ana, whose face had turned a gray shade of white, said something like, "Well, I . . . what's he . . . can't believe you'd keep . . . almost destroyed my . . ."

"It's good to see you, too," Giancarlo responded confidently.

Ana regained her composure when she said to Mom, "I'd never let someone I fired come back into my salon. You couldn't just mail him his check?"

Mom shrugged, concentrating on Ana's hair. "Giancarlo was one of my best stylists," Mom said. "He's like family."

"You mean like a family member who ruins everything?" Ana suggested. Mom ignored her. "Maybe I have a better vetting process for *my* stylists.

199

Because *my* stylists would never do anything like what *your* stylist did. I'd be surprised if he could ever find a job styling again. Maybe someone will let him be the sweeper."

My face flushed hot, and I stopped what I was doing (you know—*sweeping*). Mom stopped what she was doing, too. She turned Ana's chair until she could look her directly in the eyes and said, "Mickey, did you go on any interesting walks this week?"

This is what she wanted from me! I stepped over to her station, broom in hand, and said, "Yes, I went for a walk this week."

Ana eyed us both like she knew what was coming. "Yes, Chloe. I saw your daughter out after dark with some boy on a deserted street. I have to say, I'm surprised you'd allow such an unsupervised excursion. Doesn't seem safe but that's just me." Giancarlo took a step toward Mom's station—just a step, nothing more. He kept his eyes on us and I swore I could see beads of sweat building on Ana's temples.

"You were out with Giancarlo," I said to her. "I saw you coming from The Kitchen."

She shrugged like it was no big deal, but her face gave her away. "He wanted some advice on moving to bigger salons in bigger cities. I was just being nice."

"Not true," Giancarlo said. "You offered me a job at your salon."

I gasped. She really had been trying to steal him from us all this time. How could she!

"It seems odd to me," Mom said, turning her attention back to what she was doing to Ana's hair, "that you would offer him a job one day, and then the next sit in his chair and for the first time in his entire career, he supposedly does a poor job?"

"He . . . he was trying to take revenge on my hair."

"Revenge because you offered him a job?" Mom asked. "That doesn't make sense."

"I don't know what kind of crazy thoughts you small-town people have," she said, a bit desperately.

"Hmm . . ." Mom muttered. "Why don't you tell us about that great article you were reading as you sat beneath the hair dryers. You know, the one that was so fascinating you couldn't tear yourself away?" She glanced at Ana in the mirror, who was literally slumping down in the styling chair like maybe she could disappear. "It's odd that an experienced stylist and colorist wouldn't know how important time is when setting a color job. Isn't it?"

"He was responsible," Ana said quickly. "It wasn't my fault." Her eyes darted around and she said, "I'm uncomfortable—I don't want you doing my hair anymore." She made a move to get up but Mom gently patted her shoulder.

"Ana, it's okay," Mom said. "I know about your

salon. I know what troubles you've been having."

"My salon is just fine," Ana said defiantly.

"That's not what the article Mickey found last night said." Mom leaned on the back of the chair and looked at Ana with sincerity. "It's hard running a business. I understand. And I'm sorry you've fallen on hard times but—"

"Don't even," Ana said, sitting up straight as if getting her confidence back. "Don't you even start being patronizing toward me. You are not a friend of mine, so don't pretend to comfort me and act like you care, because you proved that you don't."

"Ana," Mom said, "what are you talking about?"

"Us!" she said. "We were supposed to start a business together! Or did you forget? That was our plan right out of beauty school and then you just ditched me."

"I got an internship," Mom said. "And so did you!"

"Oh, sure, my internship was great," Ana said sarcastically. "In some basement salon with bad lighting and beauty-school dropouts."

"I don't understand," Mom said, and I wanted to say, "Yeah, me neither." "What does some internship years ago have to do with what you're doing here in town this week?"

"Because you're the best! You always have been! You got on some TV show even though you don't need the help. Do you know how many times I've applied to *Cecilia's Best Tressed*? At least five. And you get in just like that. Then, as if you need any more exposure, you get a write-up in that blog! Everything is just handed over to you, Chloe. It all comes so easily for you. It's not fair. All I need is one good stylist and my salon is back on track. And if I couldn't convince Giancarlo to come work for me by offering him more money in a bigger market, then I had to do something to make him want to work for me. And when a stylist has no job, they start looking a little more closely at whatever is coming their way. So *that's* what I did."

We all just stood staring at her. When I say all of us I mean just about the entire salon. I couldn't believe she'd done all of this, let alone admit to it.

"Oh, Ana," Mom said. "All these years you've felt this way. Why didn't you say something? You never even contacted me."

"You were too busy to be contacted," Ana said bitterly, yet on the verge of tears.

Mom looked at her sadly. "Come on," she said. "Let's go back to my office to talk."

Ana kept her chin firmly up as she stood from Mom's styling chair and followed her back to her office. Just before Mom shut the door, she said to Giancarlo across the salon, "Better get back to your station. Clients have already been asking about you. Any walk-ins will be happy to have you."

Giancarlo beamed. "Thanks, Chloe."

When Mom shut the door, the stylists (and even the clients) let out sighs of relief. I practically raced over to Giancarlo.

"It worked!" I said, bouncing on my feet. "I can't believe she totally confessed!"

"Yes, I know," he said.

Devon came over and said, "Glad to have you back. I had to style Mrs. Henkins yesterday in your absence. That one's a piece of work."

"Did she insist on using a ruler to make sure her bangs were straight?" he asked.

"Sure did," Devon said.

Giancarlo smiled. "I've been doing her hair for so long I'm used to it. I'll call her and let her know I'm back. As for you," he said, looking down at me. "I owe you a huge thank-you. I heard you've been my biggest cheerleader all along."

I blushed, embarrassed that he knew I'd been defending him.

"I just want to say thank you, Mickey," he said. "You never doubted me for a moment and that means a lot to me."

I wanted to tell him he's the best stylist at the salon and my favorite person there, but I didn't want to say it in front of the others. Even if it was obvious I didn't want to admit to playing favorites. As the owner's daughter I had to stay professional, you know.

"You're welcome," I said.

"And if there's anything I can do for you," he said, setting up his station, "you let me know."

Just then the door chimed and in walked Eve and Marla. After all the excitement, I realized I hadn't come up with a plan for fulfilling the promise I made to Eve about getting her hair styled.

"Well," I began, "there is one thing you can do for me."

CHAPTER 20

There was one thing left to do that evening and that was get ready for the dance.

I first met Eve when she came into the salon for an appointment with Giancarlo, so I loved that she was his first client after the last crazy few days.

"She's in good hands," Giancarlo told me as Eve got settled in his chair.

"I know she is," I said. "Thanks, Giancarlo, for doing this. It means a lot."

"Oh, stop it," he said. "You know I can't say no to you."

Turning back to Eve, his tools and products ready to go, Giancarlo said, "It's been a few days since I worked. I hope I'm not too rusty."

Eve looked at me nervously until I said, "He's joking! Giancarlo, be nice."

"Scoot out of my space," he said. "Shouldn't you be

getting your own hair done?"

"I will, but I have to do something else first."

I had told Eve I'd do Marla's hair, and once they all decided to go to the dance Marla decided she'd like to take me up on that offer. That meant I wouldn't have time for a blowout done by Mom. It was fine, though, really. I was more interested in seeing my friends look good and have a fun night, especially after the stressful week.

Mom let me work on Marla's hair in the break room, away from the clients.

"Just stay away from any dyes and other products," she said with a wink.

The thing with Ana had gone about as well as anyone could hope it would, so now everyone was relaxed and happy, just the way Hello, Gorgeous! should be.

"I honestly didn't think much about it once I left school and we slowly began to lose touch," Mom told me and Giancarlo. "That was my fault for brushing it off, but I certainly wish Ana would have come to me a lot sooner—*years* sooner—to tell me how she felt. Now all these years and all that negative energy, wasted," Mom said. "Could have saved ourselves a lot of trouble."

Back in the break room, I got started on Marla's hair. Even though it was short, it had long layers and I knew there was a lot of cool stuff I could do with it. She had on the first dress she'd originally held up for Eve at the store—the electric yellow, asymmetrical number—and it looked really cute on her.

She noticed me looking and said, "You were right. I guess I was thinking about myself when I spotted this dress."

"It looks really good on you," I said, because it did. It was a tough color to pull off but she did it. "I think I know just the hairstyle to go with it. You sure you trust me with this?"

"I guess I'll find out when you're done," she said.

"So this is my test, huh?"

"No," she said. "I don't mean it like that. I'm not trying to make you jump through hoops, Mickey."

I did Marla's hair in a way that looked messy and thrown together but actually took me a while to get just the right look. Violet let me use a lime-green hair extension that complemented the yellow dress—just one—and I tucked it into Marla's hair so it peeked out just a little bit. It made a nice accent in her punk hair.

"Mickey, I love it," Marla said, checking herself in the mirror. "Eve was right—you're a master at hairstyle."

I smiled. "Thanks. You have great hair—that's half the battle."

"But what about you?" she asked. "Everyone's

going to be here soon."

"Jonah and Kyle are meeting all of us here?" I asked.

"Yeah, I think so," Marla said.

Kyle was pretty vocal about not going as a group. I didn't want him to think that I had planned this so that we wouldn't be able to go alone.

"What about your hair?" Marla asked again. "I mean, it looks good now, but I didn't take up your prep time, did I?"

"No, don't worry about it," I said while trying to think what I could do to keep my promise to Kyle.

For once in my life, my hair was the least of my problems.

CHAPTER 21

I have to say, the three of us looked pretty gorgeous. Marla totally pulled off the yellow asymmetrical dress with punk hair, and the little bit of green in her hair gave it the perfect pop. Eve's hair looked like a fairy tale, all big curls flowing down her back in a half updo. The dress she'd bought was the one Marla and I had agreed on—palest pink with spaghetti straps and a belted waist.

As for me, Mom twisted my hair and piled it on top of my head in a messy but fancy do. I put on a dash of pale pink blush with a hint of shimmer, some mascara, and lip gloss—designed to enhance my look, not ward off possible kisses. I was ready to go. My dress was grass-green, belted like Eve's but pleated.

I'd texted Kyle to let him know that I just found out that Eve, Jonah, and Marla were all meeting at the salon. I hoped he didn't think I was setting him up. He texted back that it was okay, but I wouldn't really know if he meant it until he and Jonah arrived. I texted Lizbeth and she and Matthew were still on to meet us at school after their dinner. I wondered if maybe Kristen had changed her mind about being a third wheel.

That made me feel bad for her, so I decided to text her, just to make sure she was okay.

Last call for dance hall

She didn't write back.

I changed into my dress in Mom's office, and when I came out to wait in the back with Marla, Eve pulled me aside and said, "Wait, can I tell you something first?"

"Yeah, sure," I said.

"Listen, I know things have been not great between us," she said.

"Eve, that's all my fault," I said. "I'm really sorry for all I—"

"No," she said, shaking her head. "If I hear you apologize one more time." She looked at me and said, "I mean that in the nicest possible way. I just mean, I know it's been really weird between us this week, with Marla here and us being sort of friends and sort of not. I just want you to know that—it's fine."

"It's fine?" I asked, meaning *what* is fine?

"I mean, if it's okay with you," she said, "I'd like to be friends again. *Real* friends, not this sort of, kind of, maybe not really friends."

I smiled. "I'd like that."

"Whatever happened is all in the past. Okay?"

"Okay," I said, relieved.

"And thank you for being such an amazing friend to Marla this week," she said. "That meant a lot to me. Especially taking her out with you last night. That was, like, above and beyond."

"It was no big deal," I said. "I'm glad we did it. She's a good friend to you."

"Yeah," Eve said. "I've missed hanging out with her. It's been good having her here this week, even if it's made things a bit stressful."

It'd definitely been an unusually stressful week, but I had to think that at least I hadn't done anything crazy. This week, I'd been uncommonly good.

"So, you ready for tonight?" I asked.

"It doesn't feel like it's our first dance, does it?"

"Not at all," I said. "It's been stressful just getting to tonight."

"Tell me about it," she said. We walked to the back where Marla sat at the table, painting her nails a shade of brown I knew the salon didn't carry. Well, she trusted me with her hair; I guess it was only fair that she used her own polish. This time. "At least it's all working out. We're all going together, just like you wanted."

"Yeah," I said, thinking about Kyle. "The thing is—"

"Mickey!" Giancarlo's voice rang from the front. "Your date is here!"

"Oh my gosh," I said. How was I going to walk out there now? "I assume he means your date is here, too. Don't make me walk up there alone."

Eve smiled. "You got it. Did you know that Jonah is my date but I am Marla's date?"

"Oh, really?" I asked as they linked arms to walk up together.

"It's her way of making me feel like I'm not a loser or a third wheel," Marla said.

"That's not true," Eve said. "Well, maybe a little."

Marla hip-bumped her. "Thought so."

We walked through the main floor and there were the boys, looking completely out of place but also so very . . . *sigh*. At least Kyle looked so very . . . *sigh*.

"Oh my gosh, Mickey," Eve said when she saw Jonah. "He looks so cute!"

He looked fine, I supposed, but Kyle was killing it in that casual-cool sort of way wearing jeans, an un-tucked shirt, and loosely tied tie with a dark blue blazer. I noticed all the stylists and clients turning to watch us walk toward them, but they all faded away when I saw the smile spread across Kyle's face. He was happy to see me. I breathed a sigh of relief.

"Look how pretty you all look!" Giancarlo said, inspecting us as we all stood facing one another awkwardly.

"Hi," I said to Kyle. "You look nice."

He mostly looked at the floor when he said, "Thanks. Um, you look really pretty. Like, *really* pretty."

Mom came up front, all smiles and parental pride. I felt sad that Dad wasn't there, but then he appeared from the back, beaming as well. I went from sad that he wasn't there to mortified that he was in two seconds flat.

"Look at my baby girl," he said, coming up front and giving me a side hug. Mom held up a camera and snapped a photo of us. I died.

Kyle held out a box toward me and said, "I got this for you."

"A present?" I said.

He smiled. "Sort of."

Before I could even open it, Jonah said, "Dude! You didn't tell me we were doing the flower thing."

Kyle looked back at Jonah and said, "Man, some things you really need to figure out on your own."

Eve playfully swatted him. "Yeah, Jonah."

I opened the box and inside was the prettiest flower corsage I had ever seen.

Okay, it was the only one I'd seen, at least in real life. But it was beautiful. It was this big, yellow lily flower that was like a huge sunburst surrounded by little green leaves. It complemented my dress perfectly.

"It's so pretty," I said. "Thank you so much."

"Actually," he said, stepping toward me and taking it out of the box for me, "it's for your hair." He showed me the hair comb that was in the back of it. "I hope it's okay. I thought it might look nice."

I wanted to melt right there in the salon. Was there anything more thoughtful than that?

"I love it," I said. "It's perfect, Kyle." He beamed, proud at a job well done.

I went to Mom's station to use her mirror. "Want some help?" she asked me, and how could I turn her down? She fastened it perfectly. I checked myself in the mirror, seeing how well it looked with my dress.

"How did you know it'd match my dress?" I asked him.

"I had a little help," he said and nodded to Marla. That made it official—Marla was cool in my book.

"Pictures!" Mom said, clapping her hands. "Everyone together." I have to say it was rare to see her so gushy and momlike at the salon in front of her staff. For some reason it made me feel really good, even special.

We all gathered in front of the products wall to pose.

"Closer!" Mom demanded. "Everyone squeeze in."

I stood next to Kyle, of course, and he put his hand on my back. I didn't know what to do with mine, but it felt weird hanging by my side. I raised it up to sort of put on his back, too, without exactly touching him.

Look, I was doing the best I could.

"Say gorgeous!"

"Gorgeous!" we all cheered.

Once the photo portion of the night was done, we were ready to head out.

Since the school was so close, we decided to walk over even though Dad offered us a lift.

The five of us started out and we hadn't made it far before Kyle said to me, "Hey, mind if we take a little detour?"

"No," I said, wondering what it meant. Would this be the moment? "Whatever you want."

"Guys, we're going to go this way," he said, pointing to a trail that led across the park. The school was on the other side, a little roundabout but scenic nonetheless.

"Okay," Jonah said with a wave. "See you there."

Eve gave me a smile and a wave, and Marla gave me this funny smile that I think was meant to tease me for being alone with Kyle.

"I hope you don't mind," Kyle said. "I know it seems like a small thing, but I really just wanted to go to the dance alone with you."

"No, it's totally fine," I said. "Eve texted me at the last minute. I really had no idea they were going tonight."

"I know," he said. "Jonah told me."

I smiled. I was glad we were walking into the dance together, alone. It made it feel more official somehow. Maybe that's what he wanted, too.

As we walked across the park, Kyle reached over and took my hand in his. It wasn't the first time we'd held hands, but it felt more real this time. Maybe because we were dressed up and going to our first-ever dance. It felt like the first time I really truly thought of him as my boyfriend.

When we walked through the doors of the school gym, lights were flashing and the music was loud and thumping. The place was pretty full, so I guessed we'd come at just the right time. I scanned the gym for our friends, then wondered if he wanted us to stay alone all night. Would we hang out with our friends at all?

A slow song came on almost immediately, and it was like the DJ dude was forcing us to get close right off the bat. Kyle stood for a moment, watching the other couples go to the dance floor.

"So," I said, watching the other couples. "Want to dance?"

"Sure, yeah," he said. "I was going to ask you."

And this time, I took his hand and we walked together

to the dance floor. He put his arms around my waist, resting his hands on the small of my back, and I rested mine on his shoulders, dangling just behind his neck. I wanted to kick myself for not brushing my teeth before leaving. I hoped my breath didn't stink.

Over Kyle's shoulder I saw a couple totally making out, right there on the dance floor. Just as I wondered if the teachers and chaperones would allow that, Ms. Carter came over and pulled them apart. When I saw their faces, I started laughing.

"What?" Kyle asked, turning his head slightly to look at me.

"Over there," I said, turning our bodies slightly so he could see. "I guess Tobias and Kristen are back together. They just got busted kissing."

"Seriously?" he asked, a laugh in his voice.

"Like, legitimately macking down," I said.

"I can't believe I'm even surprised by that."

"I know," I said. "I guess it's just one of those things we'll never understand."

"I'm not sure I'd want to understand that."

The song faded and a faster song came on. As we moved off the dance floor, we ran into Jonah, Eve, and Marla.

"Come on," Eve said, grabbing my hand. "Let's all go dance!"

I let her pull me but before I could get too far I

reached back and pulled Kyle in with me. Soon we were all dancing, not caring what we looked like or how cheesy the song was. Lizbeth and Matthew joined us, and they looked like the perfect preppy couple, both matching in nautical-blue and white. Later, Kristen and Tobias joined us, claiming they almost got kicked out of the dance "for no reason," and Kyle said, "Yeah, we saw you guys doing absolutely nothing."

"I think the whole school did," I said. It got a smile out of Kristen.

"Gonna get me some more of that later on," Tobias said, grabbing Kristen's waist.

"Ugh, why are you so nasty?" she snapped, swatting his hand away.

"What?" Tobias asked. "What'd I do?"

"Hey," Kyle said to me as Kristen laid into Tobias about how disrespectful he was. "Want to go outside for a minute? Get some air?"

"Perfect," I said.

We went out the door we'd come in. Some people were already starting to leave even though there was still a half hour left in the dance. I couldn't believe it was almost over. It seemed like we just got there.

We stepped a little away from the door, just out of the light of the sidewalk lamp. I leaned against the wall, feeling the cool brick against the top of my back and through my dress. A light breeze blew across my face, and I closed my eyes, feeling it cool me down after dancing.

"Mickey," Kyle said, saying my name so gently I slowly opened my eyes. He stood in front of me and said, "I'm really glad you came to the dance with me tonight."

The voices of the other students faded. In the distance I heard a car honk.

"I'm glad, too," I said in the same quiet tone he used.

In almost a whisper he said, "I really want to kiss you."

My heart pounded in my chest. I didn't move from my position against the wall, but suddenly the coolness of the brick and the breeze across my face did nothing to help the heat that had suddenly risen all up my body. I shivered. Mustering all my courage, I said, "Then you should."

"I should?" he asked with a slight grin and raised eyebrow.

I nodded yes.

He leaned in slowly, moving his eyes from my eyes down to my lips. I only parted my lips the tiniest bit because I really wasn't sure what was supposed to happen but hoped that he did. I watched as he closed his eyes. I closed mine, too. Suddenly, his lips were on . . . my cheek.

He pulled back quickly. "I'm so sorry. I didn't mean to—oh my gosh, I feel so stupid."

Okay, so he closed his eyes too soon and misaimed. Not a big deal. It actually made me smile because in that one little slipup I knew that this was his first kiss, too. That made me feel more self-assured.

"It's okay," I said softly. He stepped back and wouldn't look at me. Instead he glanced over to the sidewalk where kids were still leaving. I was afraid he was going to bolt with them. "Hey," I said. I reached for both his hands and pulled him closer to me, where he'd been before. Feeling brave, nervous, and superbold—and also referencing what I'd seen in some movies—I reached up for his face, holding his cheeks, and gently pulled his face close to mine. He kept his eyes focused on my lips and I kept mine focused on his. When our lips touched it was gentle, almost hesitant. I closed my eyes as he pressed his lips a little more to mine and the world disappeared once again. Lizbeth had been right—kissing was a no-brainer because at that moment, all thoughts went right out of my head. There was nothing in the world but that moment.

Until, that is, someone yelled my name.

"What are you guys doing?" Eve said, squinting through the dim light.

"Nothing," I said after we'd quickly pulled away.

I caught my breath as I said, "Just getting some air."

Kristen stood back and eyed us. She cocked her head and said, "Uh-huh. Right."

"Dude, she's like my sister," Jonah said to Kyle. "Please do not tell me you were doing what we all think you were doing."

"Okay!" I said loudly. "Nothing to see here! What do you guys want?"

"We want to leave," Eve said, holding back a laugh. "Want to go get some ice cream?"

"Sure," I said. Then I turned to Kyle. "Well, only if you want to."

"Sounds good to me," he said, holding out his arm for me to hook mine through. I accepted.

"So let's go," Kristen said. "Before you two are the next to get busted by Ms. Carter."

I'm sure I blushed, but in the dark no one saw. I was pretty sure that Kyle had blushed, too, but something about our blushing together made it okay. I knew girls told each other just about everything and I was really happy to have my friendship with Eve back. Happy even to have made a new friend with Marla, even if she didn't live here. But I wouldn't tell them about my and Kyle's first try at kissing. There are some things a girl should keep from even her best friends in the whole world. Even if you're lucky enough to have so many good ones, like me.